# 100+
## no-sew fabric
## crafts for kids

- Hours of Fun, Oodles of Projects
- Gifts, Toys, Playful Decorations & More!

MARY LINK

C&T PUBLISHING

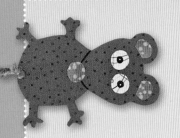

**Publisher:** Amy Marson

**Creative Director:** Gailen Runge

**Editors:** Maria Capp and Kesel Wilson

**Technical Editor:** Susan Nelsen

**Copyeditor/Proofreader:** Wordfirm Inc.

**Cover/Book Designer:** Kristen Yenche

**Page Layout Artist:** Happenstance Type-O-Rama

**Production Coordinator:** Zinnia Heinzmann

**Illustrator:** Tim Manibusan

**Photography** by Christina Carty-Francis and Diane Pedersen of C&T Publishing, Inc., unless otherwise noted.

Library of Congress Cataloging-in-Publication Data

Link, Mary, 1964-

 100+ no-sew fabric crafts for kids : gifts, toys, playful decorations & more! / Mary Link.

   p. cm.

 Summary: "Over 100 no-sew projects made with fabric and fast2fuse. Includes full-size template patterns"--Provided by publisher.

 ISBN 978-1-57120-618-3 (paper trade : alk. paper)

 1. Textile crafts--Juvenile literature.  I. Title.

 TT699.L52 2009

 746--dc22

                    2008050942

Printed in China

10 9 8 7 6 5 4 3 2 1

# Contents

## A NOTE FROM THE AUTHOR

Prepare to be amazed! This book is about using fabric in new and unique ways—no sewing required. Many of the projects can literally be completed in minutes! How is this possible? *The answer is fusible interfacing.* Fabric and interfacing are the main ingredients of every project and craft in this book.

Interfacing comes in various weights. Most brands have one side that is heat fusible. However, fast2fuse, available from C&T Publishing, is a *double-sided* stiff fusible interfacing. It is the only interfacing available that is heat fusible on both sides, which makes it a fun and versatile product to work with. fast2fuse comes in two weights: regular weight and heavyweight. All the projects in this book use heavyweight fast2fuse, which can be purchased in packages or by the yard in a 28″ width.

Although fusible interfacing is commonly used for sewing projects, dozens of projects and crafts that require *no sewing whatsoever* can be made with fast2fuse and other interfacings, as you will see here. Some possibilities include coasters, costumes, cards, crowns, candy holders, castles, and more. fast2fuse is so easy and quick to use—just pick a favorite fabric and get ready to create.

# General Directions for fast2fuse

Interfacing comes in various weights. Heavyweight is extra stiff and great for toys, mobiles, and other projects that need a lot of support. Regular weight is good for a more flexible firmness. The directions for use are quick and easy.

**1. Cut shapes:** Draw or trace pattern shapes on fast2fuse and cut them out. Cut 2 fabric pieces ½" larger than the fast2fuse (one for each side).

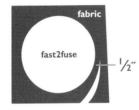

**2. Fuse the first side:** Place a nonstick pressing sheet on the ironing board. Place the fast2fuse on top of the pressing sheet. Place the fabric right side up on top of the fast2fuse and press with a hot, dry iron for 5 seconds.

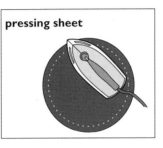

**3. Trim:** Trim the fabric edges even with the fast2fuse.

**4. Fuse the second side:** Turn over the project. Place a second piece of fabric on top of the fast2fuse and press with a hot, dry iron for 5 seconds.

**5. Trim:** Trim all edges equal.

**6. Final fusing:** Repress both sides of the project for approximately 10 seconds to permanently fuse the fabrics.

## SHORTCUTS

**Shortcut 1:** Fuse fabric to both sides of a large rectangle of fast2fuse. Trace the pattern shape onto the rectangle. Cut out the pattern shape.

**Shortcut 2:** Same as Shortcut 1, except sandwich the fast2fuse rectangle between a large folded piece of fabric. The idea is to keep the finished folded edge when cutting out the pattern.

**Shortcut 3:** Use this method when two finished edges are desired (as in belts, headbands, etc.). Trace and cut out the desired patterns on fast2fuse. Wrap fabric around the fast2fuse so that it meets or overlaps in back. Fuse both sides. Trim the overlapped fabric or use fabric glue to secure any loose edges.

# Supplies

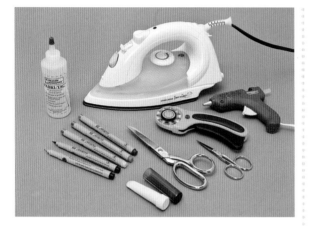

**fast2fuse:** Double-sided, stiff fusible interfacing in regular and heavyweight

**Fabric:** 100% cotton

**Iron:** The dry heat of the iron is what causes the glue of the fusible interfacing to fuse and bond with the fabric.

Kids should use an iron or low-heat glue gun only with adult supervision.

**Nonstick pressing or appliqué sheet:** Use this sheet under the project while fusing. Baking parchment paper can act as a substitute.

**Fabric markers:** These markers do not bleed onto fabric. They are excellent for adding small details.

**Low-heat glue gun and fabric glue:** Useful for adding details to projects and for securing embellishments. Although fabric glue works well for some projects, you may find that you prefer a low-heat glue gun for other projects. It is mostly a personal preference.

**Fusible appliqué web:** Used for many appliqué techniques. A hot iron fuses the web to the fabric. The fabric can then be cut and applied to a base fabric, where it is fused again into a permanent position.

**Clear acrylic varnish or sealer:** Use as a finish to cut down on fraying or to give a project a glossy finish. It is perfect for jewelry or heavily used items.

**Marking, tracing, and cutting tools:** These include rulers, scissors, rotary cutters and mats, templates, and tailor's chalk or marking pens.

**Embellishments:** Pom-poms, ribbons, rickrack, buttons, glitter, cording, yarn, googly eyes, chenille strips, grommets, or even found objects are great for embellishing projects.

Remember not to add embellishments to any item that a toddler or infant will be handling or playing with, as the embellishments can come off and be swallowed accidentally.

# Fabulous Flats

Turn little scraps of fabric into tiny treasures for refrigerators, lockers, gift bags, or books. Who wouldn't want to curl up with a good book and one of these fun pressed pals? Make one for a teacher, make one for a friend, and don't forget to make one for yourself. What a great way to use scraps!

# Bookmarks, Tags, and Magnets

## MATERIALS

- Pattern-sized rectangles of heavyweight fast2fuse
- Fabric scraps
- Fusible appliqué web or fabric glue
- Embellishments, such as glitter, buttons, chenille strips, and fabric markers (optional)
- Fancy yarn or ribbon (optional)
- Paper punch (optional)
- Magnets (optional)

## INSTRUCTIONS

*All patterns for this chapter are on pages 14–20. Use a copy machine to enlarge the patterns 125%.*

*See General Directions for fast2fuse, page 4, for fusing directions.*

**1.** Use Shortcut 1, page 5, to fuse the body fabric to the fast2fuse rectangle.

**2.** Trace the desired pattern onto the fabric and cut out the shape.

**3.** Use fusible appliqué web and fabric markers to add detail as desired. For patterns with a lot of detail, such as the fairy on page 16 or the dog on page 14, fuse the base body fabric and then layer the details on top. Make an extra copy of the desired pattern, then cut apart the detailed pieces to use as your fusible appliqué patterns.

**4.** Add embellishments of your choice (remember that bookmarks should be flat).

**5. To finish as a bookmark with a tail or tassel:** Punch a hole in the desired spot with a paper punch. Loop yarn through the hole and tie, making the tail or tassel as long as desired.

**To finish as a gift tag:** Glue a ribbon to the back of the project or tie a ribbon through a hole made with a paper punch. Use a thin fabric marker (spot test first) to add any words.

**To finish as a magnet:** Glue magnets to the back of the project.

Cards made by Mary Link and Beth Leonadis.

 mall rectangles of fast2fuse are blank canvases ready for an artist's touch. Layer on the embellishments and have fun!

# Postcards and Greeting Cards

## MATERIALS

- 4″ × 6″ rectangle of heavy-weight fast2fuse (for a typical postcard)

  OR

- 8″ × 6″ rectangle of heavy-weight fast2fuse (for a typical folded card)

- Fabric scraps

- Embellishments, such as buttons, ribbon, lace, glitter, and fabric markers

- Fabric glue

- Fusible appliqué web (optional)

- Cardstock (optional)

## INSTRUCTIONS

*See General Directions for fast2fuse, page 4, for fusing directions.*

**1.** Use Shortcut 1, page 5, to fuse fabric to both sides of the fast2fuse rectangle. If desired, glue cardstock to one side.

**2.** Decorate the card as desired. Layer on embellishments of all kinds. All the cards shown are made with basic shapes or patterns from the various projects in this book. The options are limitless.

**3.** Add wording with stamps, paint, glitter, markers, or fusible appliqué.

### Extra Fun!

Make cards of irregular shapes.

Make cards smell good by dotting them with extract or scented oil (spot test first).

Layer fused fabric for dimension.

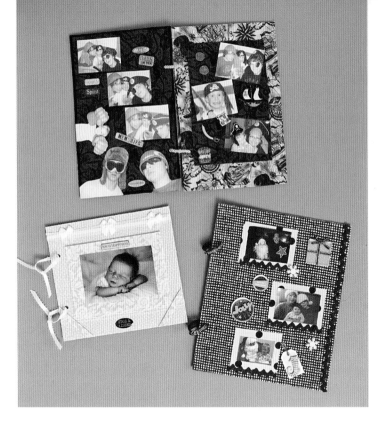

Display your favorite photos in a fabric scrapbook. Make pages of fused fabric and bind them together for a unique keepsake.

# Scrapbooks

## MATERIALS

*For 9 scrapbook pages, each approximately 9″ × 12″*

- 1 yard heavyweight fast2fuse

- 2 yards fabric (or 6 pieces of fabric, ⅓ yard each)

- Photos and embellishments of choice

- Fabric glue

- Paper punch

- 3 large 2″ metal rings (optional)

- 1 yard cording, ⅛″–¼″ diameter, for binding (optional)

- 27 grommets of desired size (optional)

## INSTRUCTIONS

*See General Directions for fast2fuse, page 4, for fusing directions.*

**1.** Measure, mark, and cut fast2fuse into pages of the desired size.

**2.** Fuse fabric to the fast2fuse pages and trim the edges.

**3.** Mark and punch holes along the binding edge. Add grommets to these punched holes, if desired.

**4.** Add photos and embellishments of all sorts. Glue in place.

**5.** Bind the book together with cording or metal rings.

### Extra Fun!

Have a party and ask each guest to design one page.

Make each page look like a quilt.

Adorn the pages with small projects from this chapter, such as a mermaid, page 11.

Spider

# Bookmarks

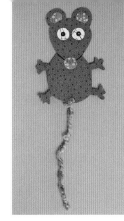
Rat

Snake

Alien

Pig

Dog

Fairy

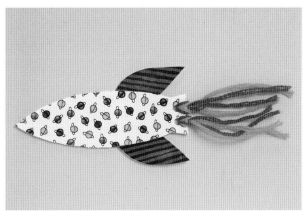
Rocket

Cow

Gnome

Dragon

Cat

## (More)
# Bookmarks

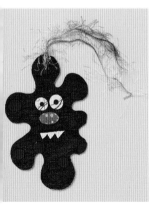

Blob

Lizard

Mermaid

Standard

# Magnets

Dragonfly

Flower

Grin

# Tags

Identification

Tree

Party hat

Leaf

Rattle

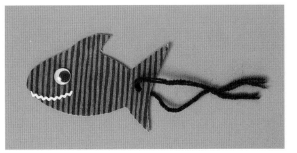

Shark

# Template
# Patterns

Snake bookmark

Dog bookmark

Standard bookmark

Flower magnet

Lizard bookmark

Rat bookmark

Leaf tag

Rattle tag

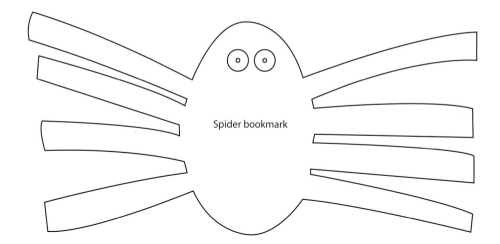

Spider bookmark

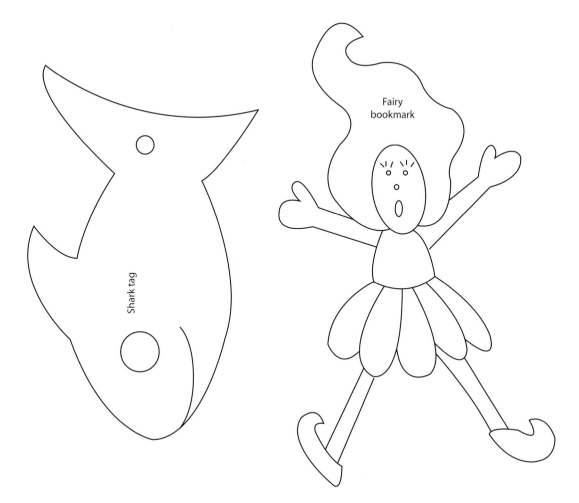

Shark tag

Fairy bookmark

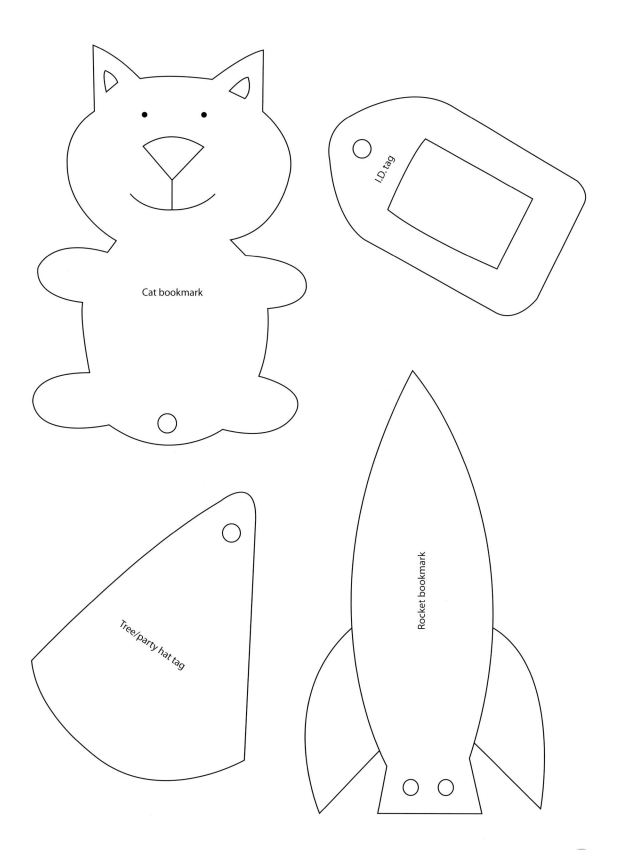

Cat bookmark

I.D. tag

Tree/party hat tag

Rocket bookmark

Gnome
bookmark

Pig bookmark

Dragon
bookmark

Cow bookmark

Blob bookmark

Alien bookmark

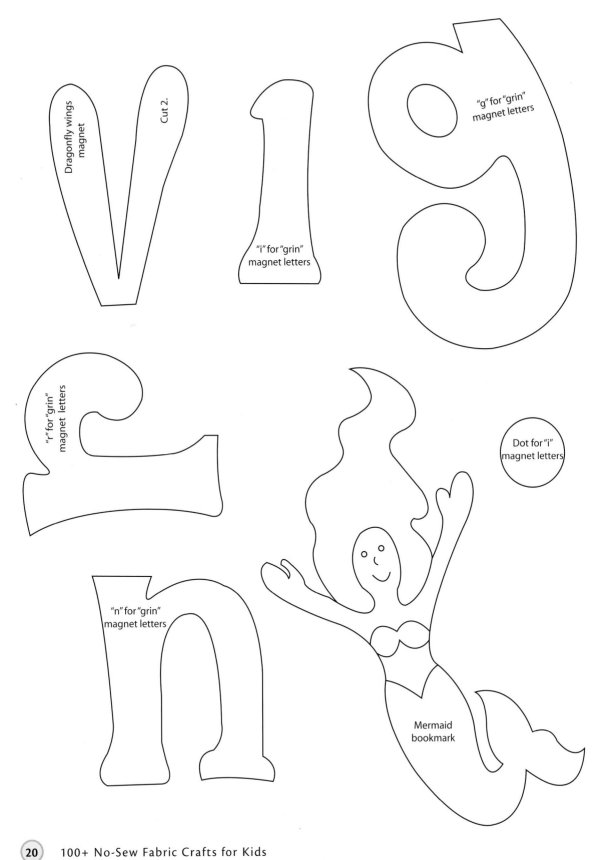

Dragonfly wings magnet

Cut 2.

"i" for "grin" magnet letters

"g" for "grin" magnet letters

"r" for "grin" magnet letters

Dot for "i" magnet letters

"n" for "grin" magnet letters

Mermaid bookmark

# Games and Toys

reate a unique puzzle with fabric. Put a different print on each side or use photo fabric to personalize the pieces. This is a great use for fabric picture panels.

# Puzzles

## MATERIALS

*For 1 puzzle*

- Rectangle of heavyweight fast2fuse in desired size

- Fabric for each side of puzzle

- Pencil or marking tool

- Water-based acrylic varnish or sealer (optional)

## INSTRUCTIONS

*All patterns for this chapter are on pages 32–41. Use a copy machine to enlarge the patterns 125%.*

*See General Directions for fast2fuse, page 4, for fusing directions.*

**1.** Use Shortcut 1, page 5, to fuse fabric to both sides of the fast2fuse rectangle.

**2.** Lightly draw puzzle shapes onto the fabric. Practice on paper of the appropriate size first or use the puzzle shapes provided.

**3.** Cut apart the puzzle.

**4.** Apply a coat of water-based acrylic varnish, if desired.

Send a puzzle as a greeting card.

Make a puzzle using cookie-cutter shapes as the templates.

Add embellishments such as glitter, yarn, or buttons to the puzzle (not for babies or toddlers).

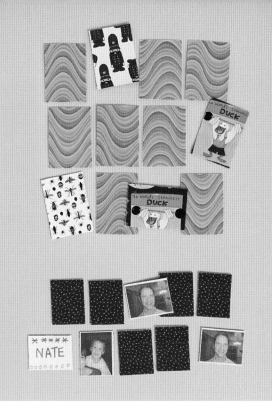

C ard games are a favorite for kids. In this common memory game, the idea is to find "matches" from a set of cards. The cards can be made in any size or quantity desired. Kids love to see pictures of themselves; photo fabric works great for making game pieces. Add letters, numbers, or words to the cards for matching. For older children, make word cards that match picture or color cards.

# Card Games

## MATERIALS

*For 1 deck of cards*

- ⅓ yard heavyweight fast2fuse
- ⅓ yard small-print fabric for the card backs
- Fabric scraps of various colors and prints for the card fronts
- Fusible appliqué web or fabric glue
- Fabric markers (optional)

## INSTRUCTIONS

*See General Directions for fast2fuse, page 4, for fusing directions.*

**1.** Fuse ⅓ yard of fabric to one side of the fast2fuse.

**2.** Decide on the size of cards and cut as many as possible from the fused fabric. A traditional playing card works well as a template.

**3.** Fuse fabric scraps to the card fronts. Make 2 of each card front, as these will be the "matches."

**4.** Trim the edges.

 How to Play

Shuffle the cards and lay them out with the pictures face down. Take turns flipping over cards, two at a time. If a match is found, the player keeps the cards. If a match is not found, the cards are flipped back over in the same place. The player with the most matches wins!

**Extra Fun!**

Put second-language words on the cards to match English words.

Make a "family" matching game.

This game promotes great memory-building skills for all ages, including nursing home residents.

Create a checker, chess, or tic-tac-toe game board out of fabric. These can be any size, from tiny stamp size to larger traditional size . . . or even bigger! Game pieces can be buttons, pom-poms, pebbles, or even beanbags.

# Game Boards

## MATERIALS

*For a 20″ traditional checker-board game*

- ⅔ yard heavyweight fast2fuse
- ⅔ yard base fabric
- ⅓ yard complementary fabric
- ⅓ yard fusible appliqué web
- Measuring tools
- Game pieces of your choice

## INSTRUCTIONS

*See General Directions for fast2fuse, page 4, for fusing directions.*

**1.** Cut a 20″ × 20″ square of fast-2fuse. Fuse the base fabric to both sides and trim the edges.

**2.** Fuse appliqué web to the complementary fabric, according to the manufacturer's directions. Measure and cut 32 squares 2″ × 2″.

**3.** Position the 32 squares in checkerboard fashion onto the large base square and fuse them into place.

Extra Fun!

Make a double-sided game board.

Make other game boards, such as backgammon.

Make games for car trips by using hook-and-loop tape to hold pieces in place.

T his fun carnival game is easy to make and to play. Follow the cone party hat directions, page 54, to make the cones. Or use beverage bottles, cans, or toys as the objects of the ring toss. Simply stand a few steps back and try to toss the rings around the objects.

# Ring Toss

## MATERIALS

*For 6 large and 6 medium rings*

- 1 yard heavyweight fast2fuse
- 2 yards cotton fabric
- Large (10″) dinner plate for template
- Medium (8″) salad plate for template
- Small (6″) dessert plate for template
- Pencil or other marking tool

## INSTRUCTIONS

*See General Directions for fast2fuse, page 4, for fusing directions.*

**1.** Use Shortcut 1, page 5, to fuse fabric to the front and back of the fast2fuse.

**2.** Trace as many large circles as possible onto the fused fabric. Cut out the circles. Trace medium circles inside the large circles and small circles inside the medium circles. Cut out the rings by folding the fabric and snipping a small starting hole on the circular trace line.

**3.** Trim all the edges.

Hold a backyard carnival or birthday party with the games.

Have players "win" whatever they ring.

Make "gold" rings for bridal shower games.

There are two ways to make the traditional fishing game. One way is to use small magnets to catch paper-clipped fish. The other (much trickier and more skill-building) way is the traditional "hook" method, in which a paper-clip hook is used to catch an upright fish. If desired, you can number the fish for keeping score.

**Extra Fun!**

Design a funny fish, a piranha, or a shark.

Use bent brown chenille strips for a "wormy" hook.

Give gummy worms as fishing prizes.

# Fishing

## MATERIALS

- ½ yard heavyweight fast2fuse
- Fabric scraps or 4 fat quarters
- Marking tool
- Small stick or dowel for a pole
- 1 yard string
- Paper clips
- Fabric markers for adding numbers and details
- Fabric glue (optional)
- Googly eyes (optional)
- Magnet (optional)
- Paper punch (optional)

## INSTRUCTIONS

*All patterns for this chapter are on pages 32–41. Use a copy machine to enlarge the patterns 125%.*

*See General Directions for fast2fuse, page 4, for fusing directions.*

**1.** Trace fish patterns onto the fast2fuse and cut out as many as possible. Upright fish (for the hook game) have a slotted fin that must also be traced and cut out. Small fish (for the magnet game) are one piece.

**2.** Fuse fabric to both sides of the cut-out fish.

**3.** Trim the edges. For the hook game, cut slots wide enough to slide the fish and fin together.

**4.** For the magnet game, simply slide a paper clip onto the fish. For the hook game, punch 3 holes along the top of each fish.

**5.** Add details to the fish as desired (eyes, numbers, etc.).

**6.** To make the fishing poles, tie one end of the string to the end of the dowel. Attach a magnet or a paper clip bent into the shape of a hook on the other end of the string. Adjust the length of the string as necessary.

T hese silly clowns are a snap to make for this old favorite game. The main body is a tube with a cone hat and flat feet for a base. Use any ball or even a beanbag to knock down these guys.

# Bowling

## MATERIALS

*For 5 clowns*

- 1 yard heavyweight fast2fuse
- ⅔ yard fabric for base
- ½ yard fabric for hat and feet
- Low-heat glue gun with glue
- Embellishments, such as pom-poms, googly eyes, and trim

## INSTRUCTIONS

*All patterns for this chapter are on pages 32–41. Use a copy machine to enlarge the patterns 125%.*

*See General Directions for fast2fuse, page 4, for fusing directions.*

**1.** For each clown, fuse body fabric to *one side only* of an 8½″ × 11″ rectangle of fast2fuse.

**2.** Trim the edges.

**3.** Roll the fused fabric into a short tube shape to form the body. Hot glue the overlapped edges of the tube securely.

**4.** Fuse the hat and feet fabric to the remaining fast2fuse. Trace the patterns onto the fabric and cut them out.

**5.** Form the cone hat. Hot glue the edges of the hat closed. Hot glue the hat to the top of the clown and the feet to the bottom.

**6.** Make the face and embellish as desired.

Write numbers on the clowns for keeping score.

Use a clown as a table center-piece for a party.

Make different expressions on the clown faces.

These number-awareness games are perfect for young learners. Players roll a die and try to be the first to build a pizza or a cone. Numbers on the pieces correspond to the numbers on the die. The cone can be built in any numerical order, but the pizza must have a 1 first for the crust, then a 2 for the sauce, and so on. This is a great use of scraps.

# Dice Games

## MATERIALS

*For 2 pizzas*

- ½ yard heavyweight fast2fuse
- 3 fat quarters for crust, sauce, and cheese
- Fabric scraps for pepperoni, peppers, and mushrooms
- Tracing tool
- Fabric markers
- Die

## INSTRUCTIONS

*All patterns for this chapter are on pages 32–41. Use a copy machine to enlarge the patterns 125%.*

*See General Directions for fast2fuse, page 4, for fusing directions.*

**1.** Trace the patterns onto the fast-2fuse (enough for 2 pizzas). Cut out the patterns.

**2.** Fuse fabric to both sides of each piece; trim.

**3.** Label the pieces on the front or back with a number (1–6).

| | |
|---|---|
| 1 = crust | 4 = pepperoni |
| 2 = sauce | 5 = peppers |
| 3 = cheese | 6 = mushrooms |

The directions for the ice cream cone game are the same as for the pizza game, using fabric scraps in 6 colors for the scoops.

**Extra Fun!**

Use the pizza in a play kitchen.

Make other stacked foods, such as hamburgers or sandwiches.

Glue pom-poms to the ice cream for more counting fun!

This is a great skill-building toy. The colorful pieces of fruit are very appealing to preschoolers, and little fingers will gain fine motor skills by lacing the string through the holes.

# Fruit Laces

## MATERIALS

*For 1 apple, 1 banana, and 1 pear*

- ⅓ yard heavyweight fast2fuse

- 3 fat quarters for apple, banana, and pear

- Fabric scraps for leaves and stems

- Colorful cording or shoelace, ⅛" to ¼" diameter—approximately 1 yard per fruit

- Fabric glue

- Paper punch

## INSTRUCTIONS

*All patterns for this chapter are on pages 32–41. Use a copy machine to enlarge the patterns 125%.*

*See General Directions for fast2fuse, page 4, for fusing directions.*

**1.** Use Shortcut 1, page 5, to fuse fruit fabric onto the fast2fuse.

**2.** Trace the fruit patterns onto the fused fabric and cut them out.

**3.** Fuse and glue the stems and a leaf to the fruit.

**4.** Punch holes for lacing.

**5.** Knot one end of shoelace or colored cording and lace it through the first hole. Wrap any fraying ends with tape to make a firm, pointed end.

Make more lacing kits from simple shapes, such as a circle or square.

Paint the project with clear acrylic varnish to increase durability.

Make fruit magnets by shrinking the patterns and attaching magnets to the back.

Make a zany zoo or a dinosaur park for a dresser top. These creatures come with slotted parts that slide together, so the critters can really come to life and stand on their own.

# Slotted Animals

## MATERIALS

*For 1 small zoo of animals*

- ½ yard heavyweight fast2fuse
- Fabric scraps for each animal
- Fabric markers (optional)
- Paper punch (optional)
- Yarn (optional)
- Fabric glue (optional)

## INSTRUCTIONS

*All patterns for this chapter are on pages 32–41 Use a copy machine to enlarge the patterns 125%.*

*See General Directions for fast2fuse, page 4, for fusing directions.*

**1.** Trace the patterns onto the fast2fuse and cut them out.

**2.** Fuse fabric to both sides of each piece and cut. Trim the edges.

**3.** Mark the slot lines and cut each slot wide enough for the animal parts to slide smoothly together.

**4.** Use a paper punch or a marker to make the eyes.

**5.** If desired, dab glue onto the slot points to permanently hold the pieces together.

**6.** Add optional yarn details, such as tails and manes.

Send a dinosaur as a birthday card. Use a fat quarter for each dinosaur.

Design and make farm animals.

Make an animal mobile.

Make a castle or a house for some tiny dolls or a doghouse for a small toy dog. Made from simple shapes that are folded together, these toys lie flat for easy storage. Try putting a holiday spin on these by creating a Christmas gingerbread house or a Halloween haunted house.

**Extra Fun!**

Make a haunted house with crooked shutters and dark fabric.

Make different-sized towers and glue them all together to make a large castle.

Make a replica of a known house.

# Houses

## MATERIALS

- ½ yard heavyweight fast2fuse
- ½ yard fabric for house
- ¼ yard fabric for roof
- Fabric scraps for details, such as shutters
- Hook-and-loop tape, 2″
- Straight-edged ruler
- Fabric glue
- Fabric markers (optional)
- Embellishments, such as beads and silk flowers (optional)

## INSTRUCTIONS

*All patterns for this chapter are on pages 32–41. Use a copy machine to enlarge the patterns 125%.*

*See General Directions for fast2fuse, page 4, for fusing directions.*

**1.** Cut 2 rectangles of fast2fuse, one measuring 8″ × 28″ for the house and the other 9″ × 12″ for the roof.

**2.** Use Shortcut 1, page 5, to fuse fabric for the house onto fast2fuse.

**3.** Trace the house pattern onto the fabric and cut it out.

**4.** Fold the cut pattern piece into the shape of a house, using a straight-edged ruler to make even creases.

**5.** Glue hook-and-loop tape to the overlapping house flaps.

**6.** Repeat Steps 1, 2, and 3 for the roof section.

**7.** Add any embellishments, such as a bead for a doorknob, fused scraps for shutters, or silk flowers for landscaping.

Follow the same directions to make a doghouse. For a castle keep, roll the castle into a tube shape and glue the edges together.

# Template Patterns

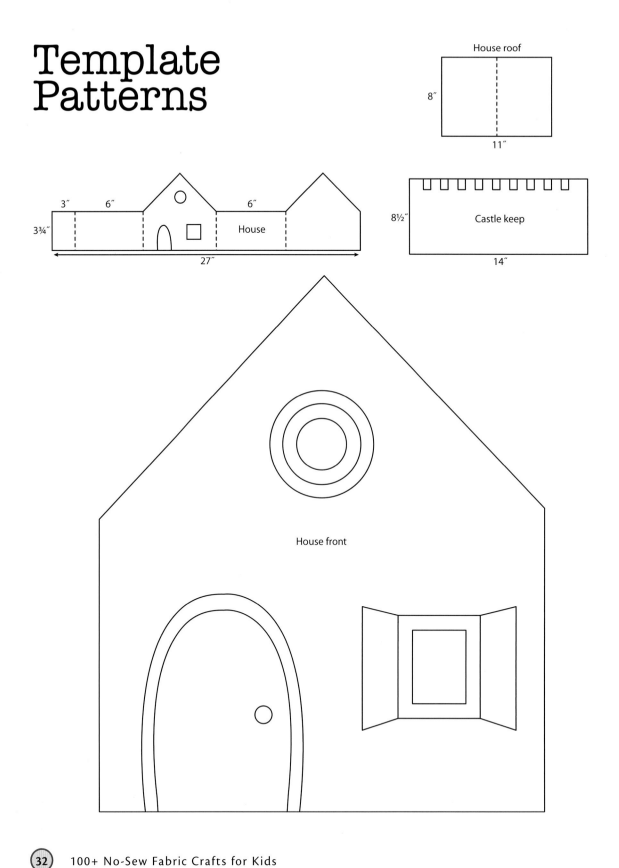

House roof

8″

11″

House

3″  6″  6″

3¾″

27″

Castle keep

8½″

14″

House front

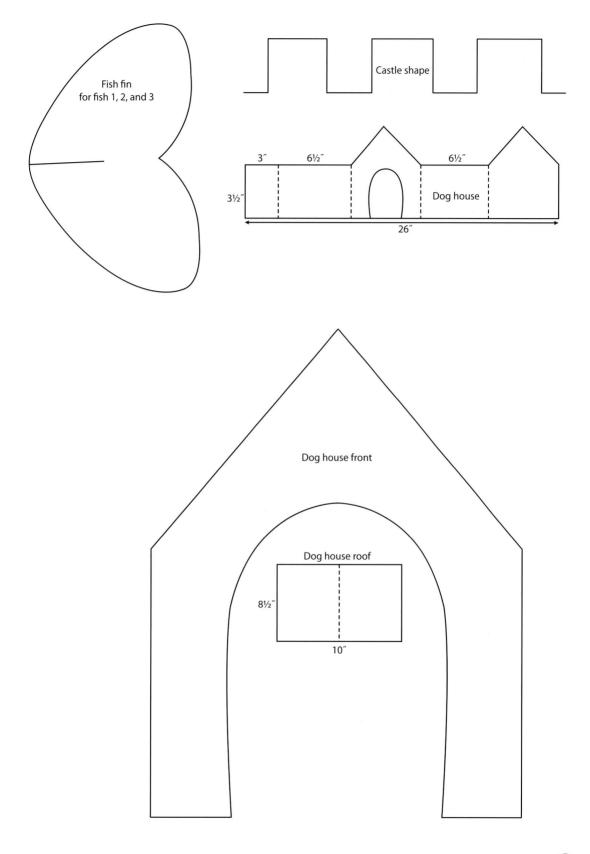

Fish fin
for fish 1, 2, and 3

Castle shape

Dog house

3"    6½"                    6½"

3½"

26"

Dog house front

Dog house roof

8½"

10"

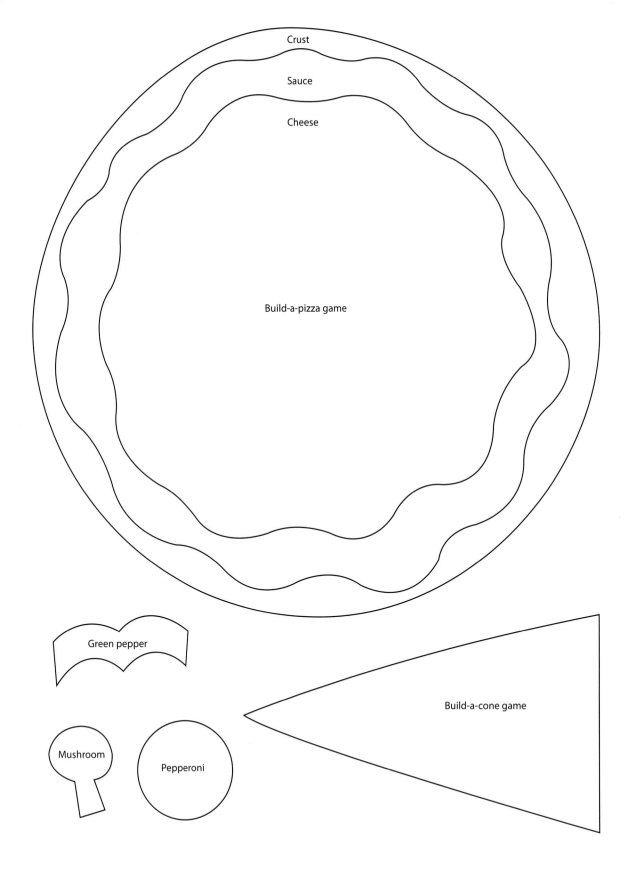

Crust

Sauce

Cheese

Build-a-pizza game

Green pepper

Build-a-cone game

Mushroom

Pepperoni

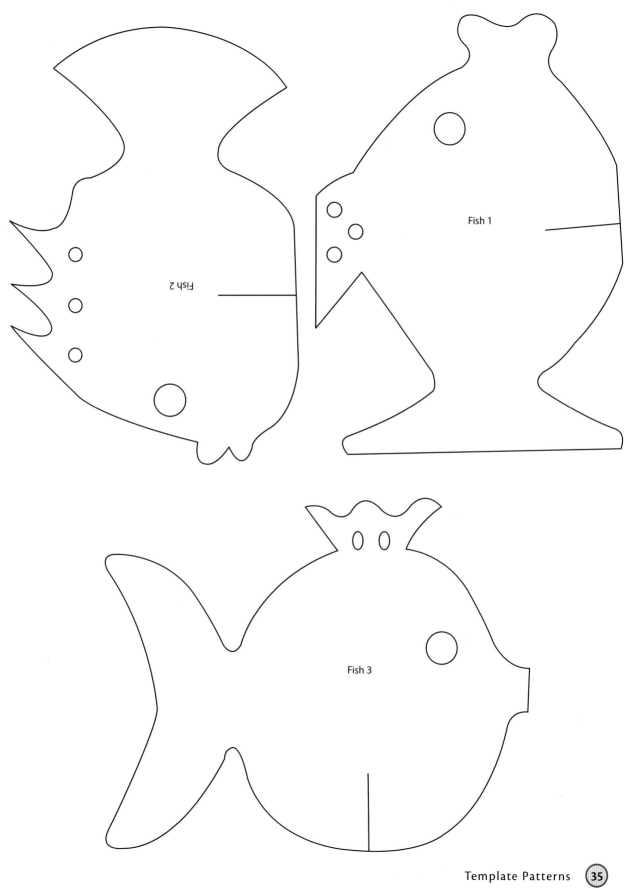

Fish 1

Fish 2

Fish 3

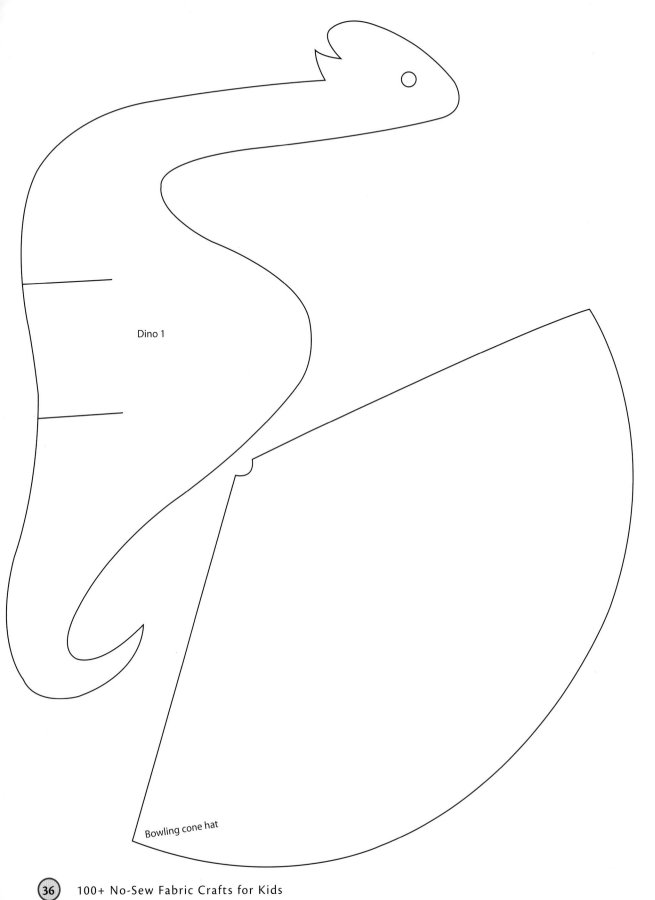

Dino 1

Bowling cone hat

Sample puzzle piece

Sample puzzle piece

Magnet fish

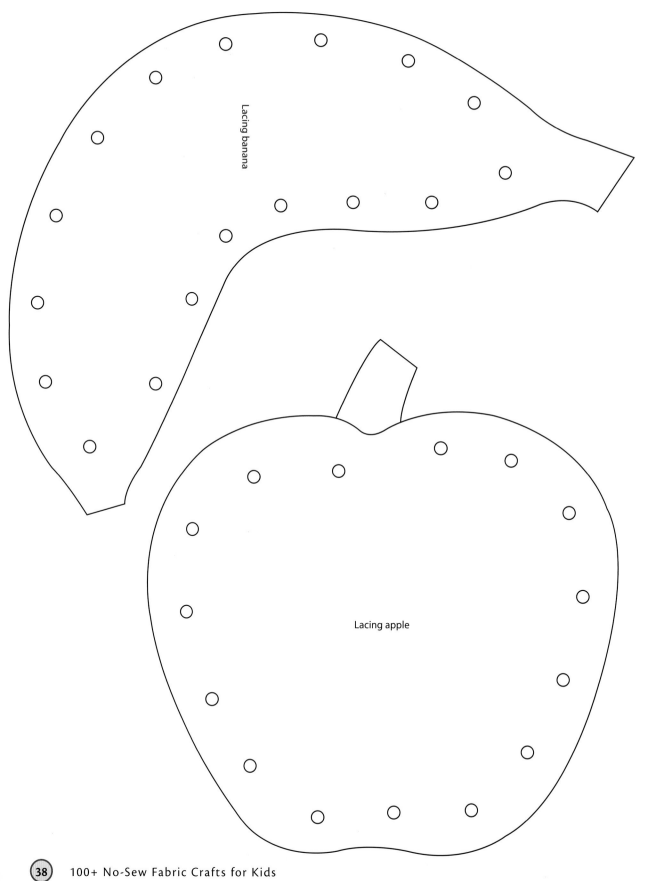

Lacing banana

Lacing apple

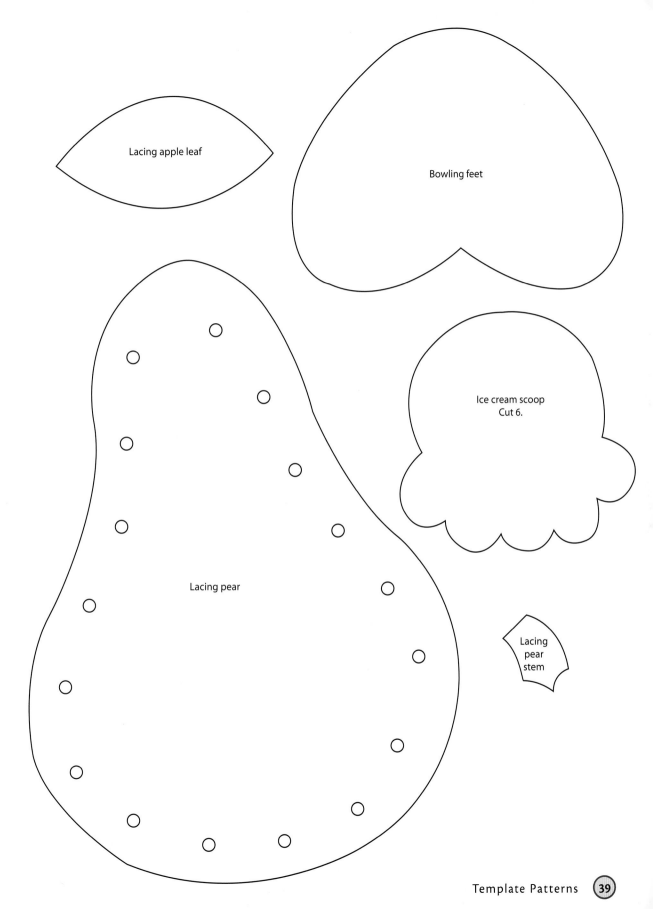

Lacing apple leaf

Bowling feet

Ice cream scoop
Cut 6.

Lacing pear

Lacing
pear
stem

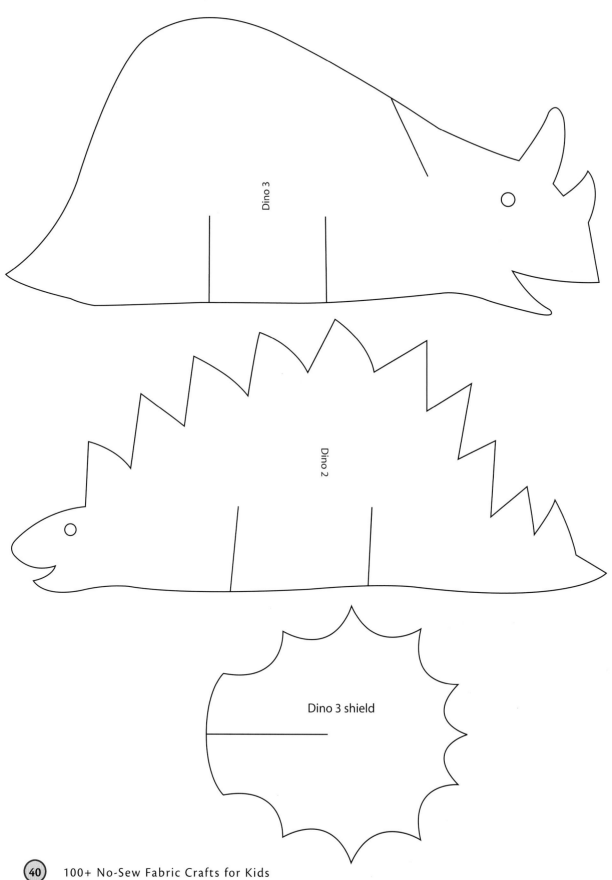

Dino 3

Dino 2

Dino 3 shield

Elephant

Ear slot

Elephant legs
Cut 2.

Lion

Lion legs
Cut 2.

Zebra

Seal

Giraffe
legs
Cut 2.

Zebra
legs

Cut 2.

Seal fin

Seal tail

Dinosaur legs
Cut 2 per dino.

Elephant ears

Giraffe

# Mobile Madness

# Doggy and Bones

Cute as can be, this dangly doggy has toys and tasty treats at his feet. This easy mobile is a fun way to brighten up a room. Try varying the lengths of the thread or using large pom-poms for balls.

## MATERIALS

- ¾ yard heavyweight fast2fuse
- ½ yard fabric for body
- ¼ yard fabric for ears, tail, and dots
- ¼ yard fabric for bones
- Fabric scraps or buttons for eyes, mouth, circles, and nose
- Invisible thread
- Fabric glue
- Paper punch

## INSTRUCTIONS

*All patterns for this chapter are on pages 49–52. Use a copy machine to enlarge the patterns 125%.*

*See General Directions for fast2fuse, page 4, for fusing directions.*

**1.** Trace and cut out the main body shape from the fast2fuse. Fuse the body fabric to one side of the fast2fuse and trim.

**2.** For added strength along the bottom of the mobile (to prevent bending), cut a 1"-wide additional strip of fast2fuse and place it along the bottom edge of the dog. This will add a double thickness to the mobile's base.

**3.** Continue to fuse the main body fabric to the fast2fuse. Trim away the excess fabric. Make sure all fabric is fused securely. Squeeze a small amount of glue into any cracks along the bottom edge, if necessary.

**4.** Use Shortcut 1, page 5, to fuse the remaining body fabric for the legs. Trace the leg patterns and cut them out.

**5.** Fuse the ear, tail, and spot fabric. Trace the patterns and cut them out.

**6.** Fuse the eye, nose, and mouth fabric. Trace the patterns and cut them out.

**7.** Position the doggy parts on the body and glue them into place. Fold the top ½" of the legs and tail inward, then glue only the top ½", so that the legs and tail stick out, giving the doggy a bit of dimension.

**8.** Fuse, trace, and cut out the bone and circle shapes.

**9.** Use invisible thread to string the bones and circles together in groups of 3 or more. Then tie these strings to the base of the dog through paper-punched holes.

**10.** To hang the mobile, attach a loop of invisible thread at the top of the dog.

## Extra Fun!

Make your doggy with his tongue sticking out.

Dangle the words **woof** or **bow wow** from the dog.

Make a pet mobile that looks like your own pet.

T he mice won't get far with this kitty on the prowl. Similar to the dog mobile, this good beginner project is sure to liven up any room.

# Cat and Mice

## MATERIALS

Same as the Doggy and Bones mobile, with yarn tails and pom-pom noses added for the mice

## INSTRUCTIONS

*All patterns for this chapter are on pages 49–52. Use a copy machine to enlarge the patterns 125%.*

*See General Directions for fast2fuse, page 4, for fusing directions.*

### Cat

Use the same basic directions as the Doggy and Bones mobile, page 43, except the cat has triangular ears and a long tail.

### Mouse

**1.** Use Shortcut 1, page 5, to fuse the mouse fabric to the fast2fuse.

**2.** Trace and cut out the pattern for the ears and body.

**3.** Mark slot lines on the ears and body. Cut the slot lines.

**4.** Slide the mouse ears into the mouse body. Dab with glue to secure.

**5.** Glue on the tail (yarn) and nose (pom-pom) and add chenille stems for whiskers.

**6.** Draw an eye dot with the fabric marker or use buttons.

Extra Fun!

Make tiny balls of yarn to hang from the cat mobile.

Hang fish from the cat mobile.

Make a black cat with dangling pumpkins.

Celebrate nature by creating a beautiful and colorful spinning mobile. The butterflies will literally flutter and dance in the air. Make a similar mobile of stars, hearts, dragonflies, flowers, or sport balls.

**Extra Fun!**

Use a different color of fabric for each side of the butterfly.

Lightly fold the butterflies so that it looks like they are flying.

Make seasonal spiral mobiles.

# Butterfly Spirals

## MATERIALS

- ½ yard heavyweight fast2fuse
- ⅓ yard fabric for vine
- Fabric scraps for a variety of butterflies
- Large (10″) dinner plate for template
- Invisible thread
- Paper punch
- Embellishments (optional)

## INSTRUCTIONS

*All patterns for this chapter are on pages 49–52. Use a copy machine to enlarge the patterns 125%.*

*See General Directions for fast2fuse, page 4, for fusing directions.*

**1.** Use Shortcut 1, page 5, to make the spiral vine. Fuse the vine fabric to an 11″ × 11″ square of fast2fuse.

**2.** Use a large dinner plate or similar-sized template to trace and cut out a large circle. Mark the center of this circle and trace a small coin at this center. Starting at the coin in the center, trace a faint spiral to the outside of the large circle edge (similar to the pattern for the mobile rocket spiral, page 49). Small imperfections will not be noticed. A tight spiral will create a long, thin vine. A wide spiral will create a short, stout vine.

**3.** Cut along the drawn line of the spiral, but do not cut out the center circle.

**4.** Use a paper punch to put a small hole in the center circle from which you will hang the mobile.

**5.** Fuse the butterfly fabric, trace the butterfly templates, and cut them out.

**6.** Use invisible thread to attach the butterflies around the spiral edges. Vary the lengths of the thread. Make holes with a paper punch and then tie on the butterflies with loops of thread. When tying on the different parts, it is helpful to hang the spiral from a doorknob or a short pole.

**7.** Hang the mobile from a ceiling hook from the hole punched in the spiral center.

**3** 2, 1, blast off! Imaginations will soar with this colorful rocket. Made from the basic shapes of a cylinder and a cone, this dimensional spacecraft is surprisingly easy and quick to make. Try hanging stars and planets with this mobile.

# Rockets

## MATERIALS

- 1 yard heavyweight fast2fuse
- Fat quarter for rocket base
- Fat quarter for cone
- Fat quarter for fins
- Fat quarter for flaming spiral
- Fabric scraps for various stars
- Invisible thread
- Low-heat glue gun with glue
- Paper punch
- Fabric markers (optional)

## INSTRUCTIONS

*All patterns for this chapter are on pages 49–52. Use a copy machine to enlarge the patterns 125%.*

*See General Directions for fast2fuse, page 4, for fusing directions.*

**1.** Use Shortcut 1, page 5. Cut a 10″ × 14″ rectangle of fast2fuse. Fuse the base fabric to **one side only**. Trim the edges.

**2.** Form a cylinder shape by gently rolling the rectangle into a tube shape. Overlap the edges by ½″ and hot glue securely.

**3.** Fuse, trace, and cut out the cone top. Roll it into a cone shape, overlap the edges slightly, and hot glue securely.

**4.** Position the cone on top of the tube and secure with glue.

**5.** Cut a 1″ × 8″ strip of fast2fuse, bend the ends, and glue this to the *inside* of the bottom of the rocket. This strip serves as a brace where the spiral flame will be anchored.

**6.** Fuse, trace, and cut out 4 fins. Cut slits into the fins. Slide them into equidistant spots around the base of the rocket.

**7.** Dab glue onto the fins to secure, if desired.

**8.** Fuse the spiral fabric, trace the pattern, and cut it out.

**9.** Fuse and cut out various scraps for sparks and stars. Use invisible thread to attach sparks and stars around the spiral's edges. Make a hole with a paper punch and tie the parts together.

**10.** Use invisible thread to tie the spiral flame to the brace glued inside the bottom of the rocket.

**11.** Attach an appropriately sized loop of invisible thread to the top of the rocket for hanging.

Use glow fabric or enhance the rocket with glow paint.

Use a fabric marker to print a child's name on the side of the rocket.

Make windows on the rocket and show someone inside (use a picture cut into a circular shape).

# Template
# Patterns

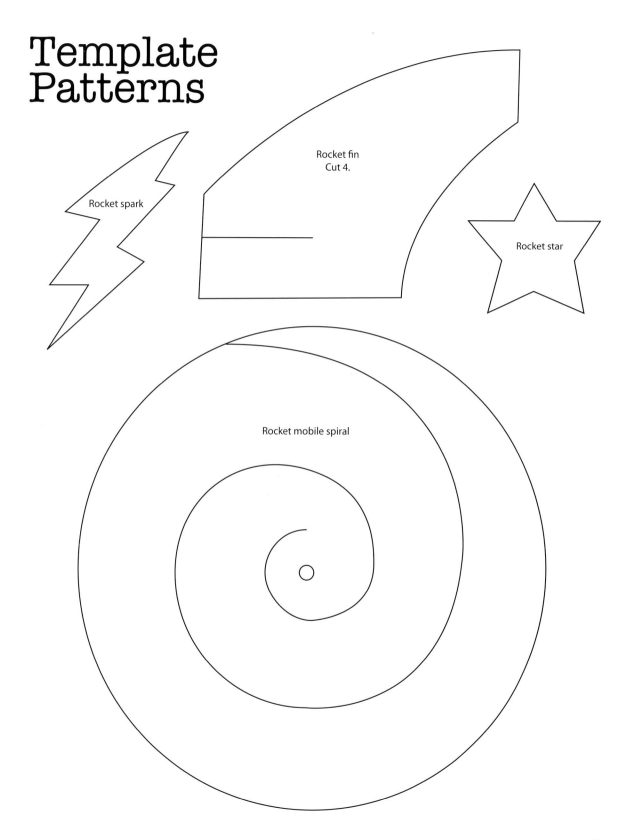

Rocket fin
Cut 4.

Rocket spark

Rocket star

Rocket mobile spiral

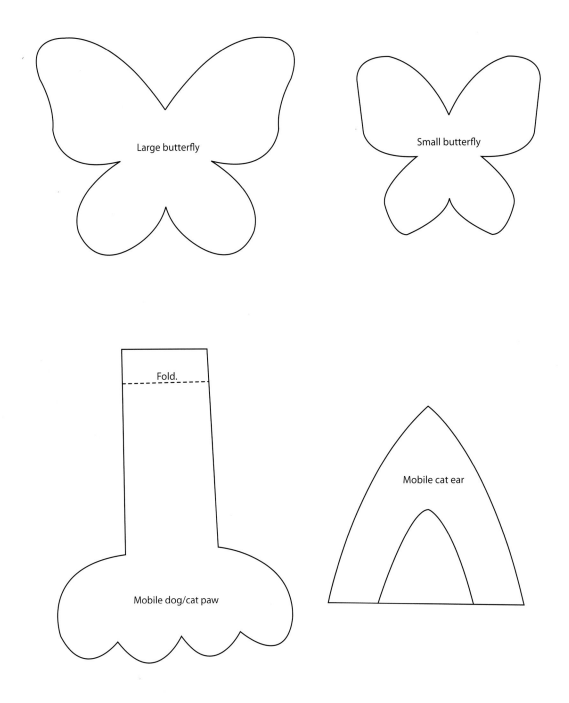

Large butterfly

Small butterfly

Fold.

Mobile dog/cat paw

Mobile cat ear

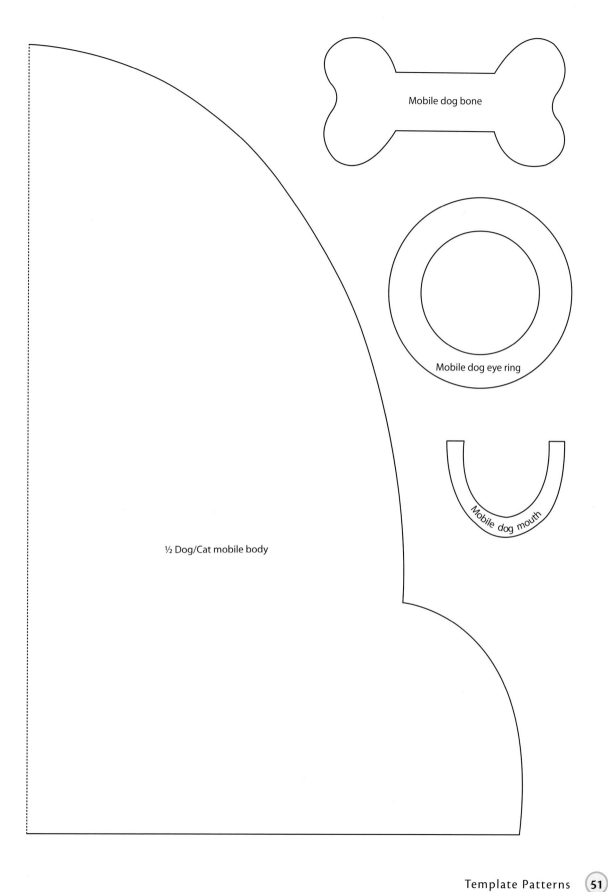

Mobile dog bone

Mobile dog eye ring

Mobile dog mouth

½ Dog/Cat mobile body

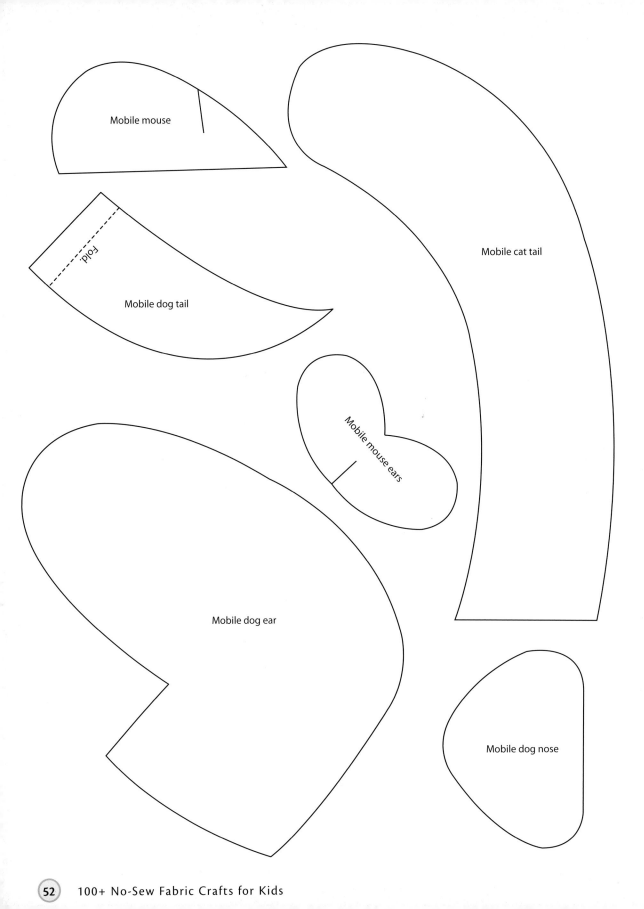

Mobile mouse

Mobile cat tail

Mobile dog tail

Fold.

Mobile mouse ears

Mobile dog ear

Mobile dog nose

Party Time

Celebrate special days with party hats. They are a snap to make. Add fringe, pom-poms, glitter, or other embellishments to spice up the party. Large cone hats can be used for wizard or princess costumes.

Glue chenille strips to the tops of the cones for an extra silly look.

Add lengths of ribbon to the princess cone hats.

Make party hats for different holidays.

# Cone Party Hats

## MATERIALS

- 9″ × 13″ piece of heavyweight fast2fuse
- 1 fat quarter
- 24″ very thin elastic
- Low-heat glue gun with glue
- Fabric glue
- Embellishments, such as rickrack, ribbons, and pom-poms

## INSTRUCTIONS

*All patterns for this chapter are on pages 61–69. Use a copy machine to enlarge the patterns 125%.*

*See General Directions for fast2fuse, page 4, for fusing directions.*

**1.** Use Shortcut 1, page 5, to fuse the fabric to the fast2fuse.

**2.** Trace the pattern and cut it out.

**3.** Roll it into a cone shape and glue the edges together. Or use a tab and slot to close the cone.

**4.** Add embellishments of your choice.

**5.** For the chin strap, tie a piece of thin elastic through holes punched in each side.

Hats should have straps of very thin, breakable elastic.

## Princess and Wizard Hats

These hats are made in the same way as the cone party hats, only larger. A 17″ × 17″ square of fast2fuse is needed, along with a larger piece of fabric. Draw an arc (as shown) to make the basic cone. Follow the directions for the cone party hats except fuse fabric to only one side of the fast2fuse. Roll the fast2fuse into a cone shape and glue securely. These hats do not require elastic straps.

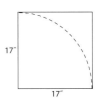

17″

17″

C rowns are not only good for parties; they are also great for playtime. Make a yummy birthday crown or play pretend with a king or fairy crown. Add jewels, glitter, ribbons, lace, and maybe even a wand or scepter!

# Party Crowns

## MATERIALS

*For 1 Birthday Cake Crown*

- ¼ yard heavyweight fast2fuse
- ⅓ yard cake fabric
- 1 yard thin cording
- Embellishments, such as rick-rack, pom-poms, and chenille strips
- Fabric glue
- 3″ hook-and-loop tape (optional)

## INSTRUCTIONS

*All patterns for this chapter are on pages 61–69. Use a copy machine to enlarge the patterns 125%.*

*See General Directions for fast2fuse, page 4, for fusing directions.*

**1.** Use Shortcut 3, page 5, to fuse fabric onto a 6″ × 24″ strip of fast2fuse.

**2.** Decorate the cake with embellishments of your choice.

**3.** Add fake candles and flames with chenille strips and scraps of fused fabric.

**4.** Size the hat to the child's head; glue the edges together. Or add a hook-and-loop strip to the inside for an adjustable hat.

## More Crowns

The king and fairy crowns use the same directions as the birthday cake crowns; however, use Shortcut 1, page 5, to fuse the fabric. Simply cut a kingly (or fairy) shape to the basic rectangle and embellish as desired.

### Extra Fun!

Have kids decorate crowns at a party.

Make an "over the hill" crown.

Have a fairy-themed party.

These happy party decorations liven up any room. A variety of fabrics can be fused on each side of the flags, perhaps different colors for different celebrations. Make small garlands for single windows or word garlands for a bedroom. Flags of all sizes are made in the same fashion. String the flags together with ribbon, cording, or fancy yarns.

# Flag Garlands

## MATERIALS

*For 12 feet of large flag garland*

- 1 yard heavyweight fast2fuse

- 2 yards fabric or a variety of scraps

- 4½ yards ribbon, cording, or fancy yarn

- Low-heat glue gun with glue

- Glitter (optional)

- Paper punch (optional)

## INSTRUCTIONS

*All patterns for this chapter are on pages 61–69. Use a copy machine to enlarge the patterns 125%.*

*See General Directions for fast2fuse, page 4, for fusing directions.*

**1.** Use Shortcut 1, page 5, to fuse the fabric to the fast2fuse.

**2.** Trace and cut out as many flags as possible from the fused fabric. By sharing edges, you can get approximately 21 flags.

**3.** Glue glitter around the edges of each flag for added pizzazz.

**4.** String flags together by gluing cording along the top edge of each flag. Hot glue works well. Or string the flags by weaving ribbon or cording through a series of holes punched along the top of each flag.

## Word Garlands

Word banners are made in the same fashion as the flag garlands, page 56. Print words on banners with stamps, stencils, markers, or paints. Create letters, names, and words or use the patterns here for ideas.

Hang letters vertically.

Make a number garland for a preschooler.

Make an alphabet garland.

These cute little boxes hide treasures and prizes of all sorts. Candy, small toys, or jewelry can be tucked inside. Surprise boxes could adorn wedding reception or other party tables. Because each box can fold into itself, no glue is needed.

# Gift Boxes

## MATERIALS

- Pattern-size piece of heavyweight fast2fuse
- Fabric scraps
- Straight-edged ruler

## INSTRUCTIONS

*All patterns for this chapter are on pages 61–69. Use a copy machine to enlarge the patterns 125%.*

*See General Directions for fast2fuse, page 4, for fusing directions.*

**1.** Use Shortcut 1, page 5, to fuse the fabric to the fast2fuse. Cut out the pattern shape.

**2.** Use a straight edge to crease along the fold lines. Tuck the box flaps closed.

**Extra Fun!**

Fuse a patchwork of fabric onto the box shape for a quilted look.

Glue on a ribbon and hang the box from a tree.

Put tiny fortunes or wishes in the boxes.

These beautiful envelopes can be made in almost any size. Simply glue along the side edges of a folded rectangle of fused fabric or punch holes along the edges and weave ribbon through the holes. Make sure to leave the top open. Anything from secret pirate notes to birthday greetings or invitations can be tucked inside.

# Gift Envelopes

## MATERIALS

*For 1 envelope*

- 5" × 16" rectangle of heavyweight fast2fuse

- 1 fat quarter

- Fabric glue

- 1 yard yarn, ribbon, or cording (optional)

- Paper punch (optional)

- Hook-and-loop tape (optional)

- Embellishments, such as lace and buttons (optional)

## INSTRUCTIONS

*See General Directions for fast2fuse, page 4, for fusing directions.*

**1.** Use Shortcut 1, page 5, to fuse the fabric to the fast2fuse rectangle. Trim the edges.

**2.** Fold the fused rectangle in half across the short width; crease. If desired, cut a small curve along the top edge of the envelope's front; use a bowl for the curve template.

**3.** Seal the edges with glue. Or, punch holes along the 2 sides and weave the sides together with cording, ribbon, or yarn. Knot or glue the ends.

**Extra Fun!** Make a folding flap for closing the envelope. To do this, increase the size of the rectangle and make the folded flap. Use a bowl as a template for making a curve on the flap. Use strips of hook-and-loop tape to close.

C elebrate with fanciful disguises. From a butterfly to a mouse, these easy masks are colorful and comfortable. Embellish with pom-poms, feathers, rick-rack, and more. These projects call for small pieces of fabric, so they are a perfect use of scraps.

# Masks

## MATERIALS

*For 1 mask*

- Mask-size rectangle of heavyweight fast2fuse

- Fabric to cover both sides of mask

- 24" thin elastic

- Fabric glue

- Embellishments, such as chenille strips and fabric markers (optional)

## INSTRUCTIONS

*All patterns for this chapter are on pages 61–69. Use a copy machine to enlarge the patterns 125%.*

*See General Directions for fast2fuse, page 4, for fusing directions.*

**1.** Use Shortcut 1, page 5, to fuse the fabric to the fast2fuse.

**2.** Trace and cut out the shapes. Fold the project in order to snip the eyeholes.

**3.** Tie elastic through tiny holes snipped on each side of the mask.

**4.** Embellish as desired.

Make a zoo of masks.

Re-create museum tribal masks.

Use broom bristles as whiskers.

# Template
# Patterns

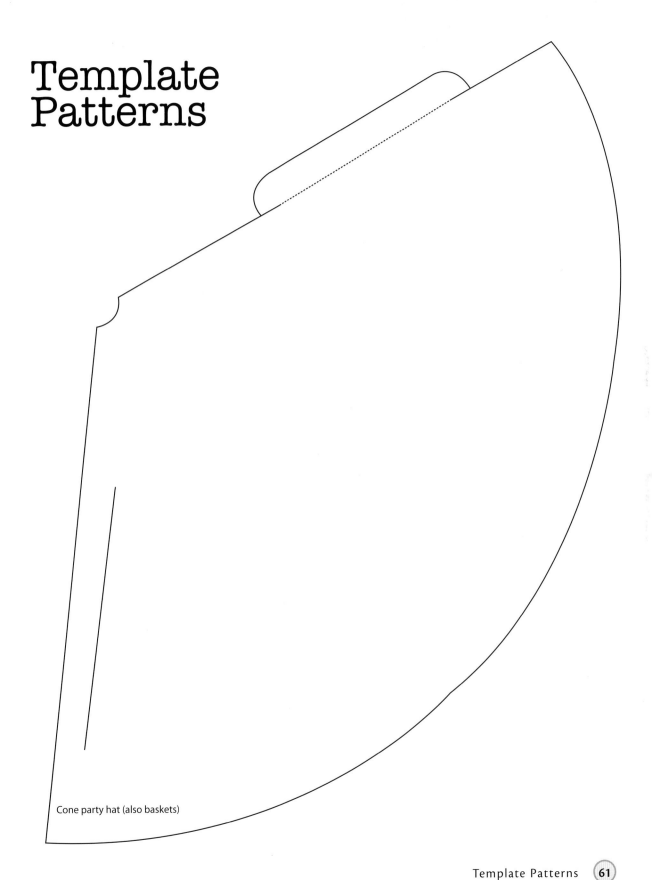

Cone party hat (also baskets)

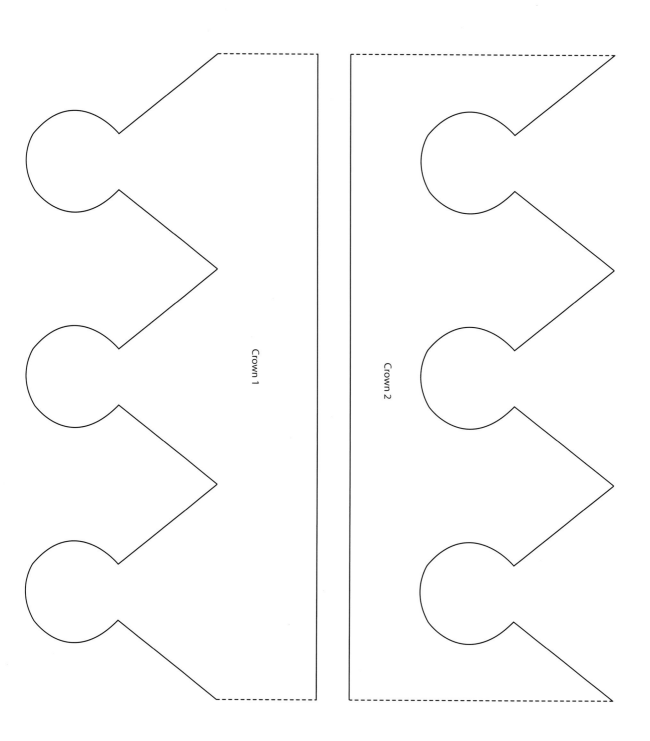

Crown 1

Crown 2

100+ No-Sew Fabric Crafts for Kids

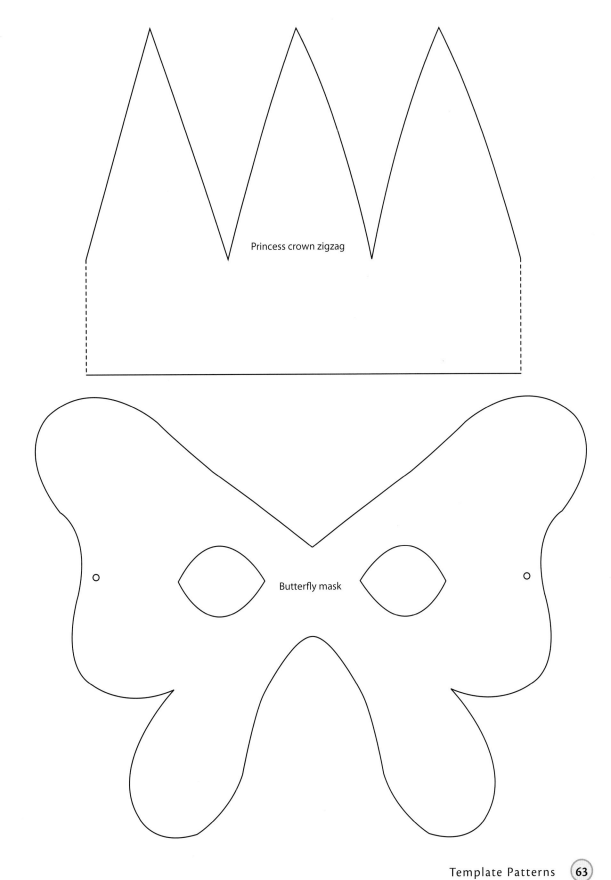

Princess crown zigzag

Butterfly mask

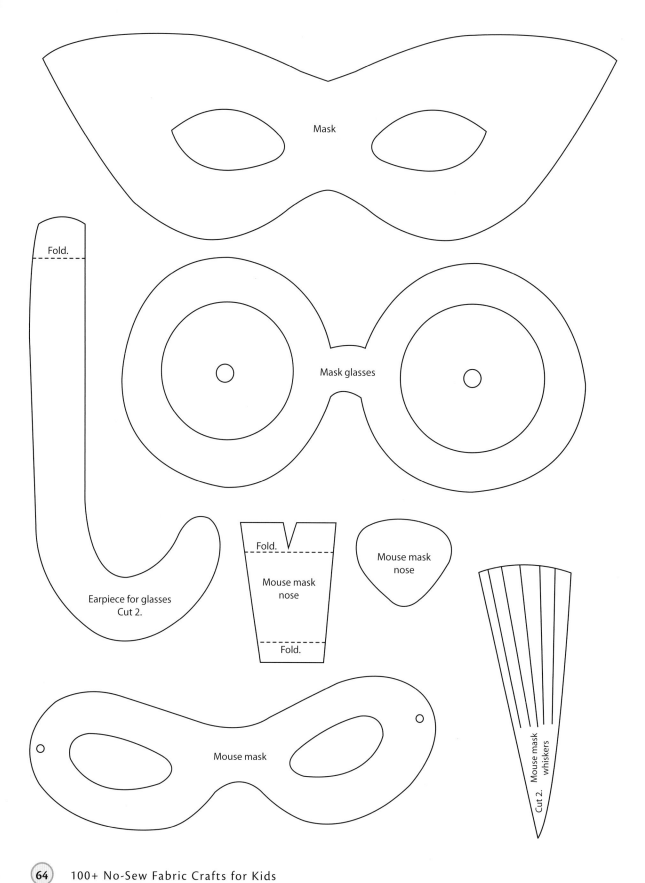

Mask

Fold.

Mask glasses

Earpiece for glasses
Cut 2.

Fold.

Mouse mask
nose

Fold.

Mouse mask
nose

Mouse mask
whiskers
Cut 2.

Mouse mask

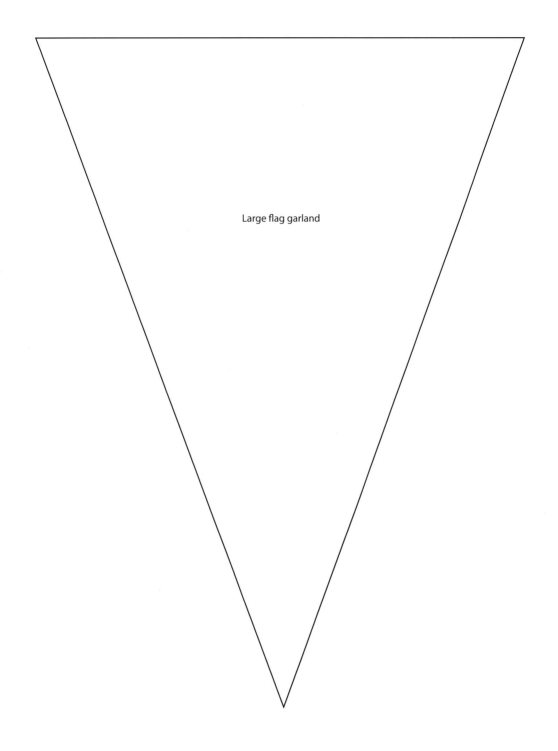

Large flag garland

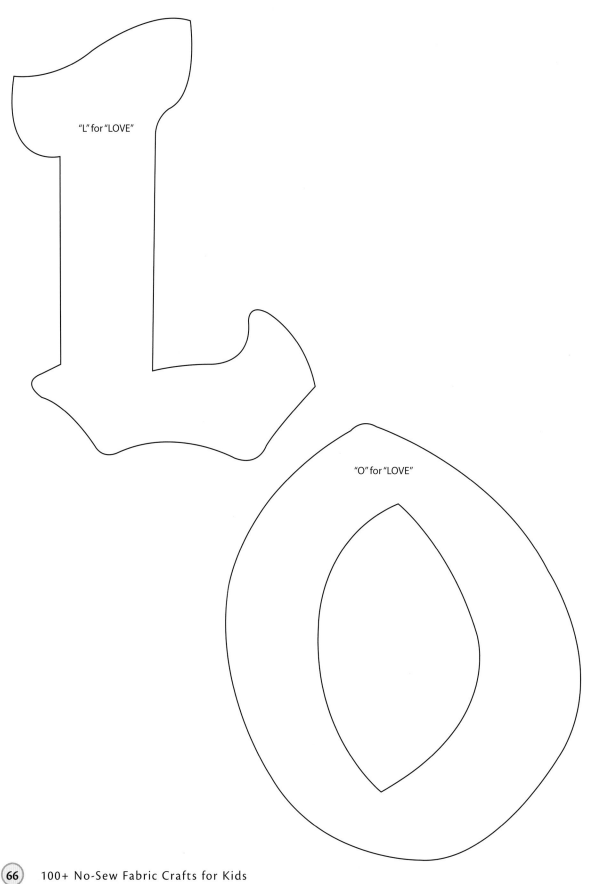

"L" for "LOVE"

"O" for "LOVE"

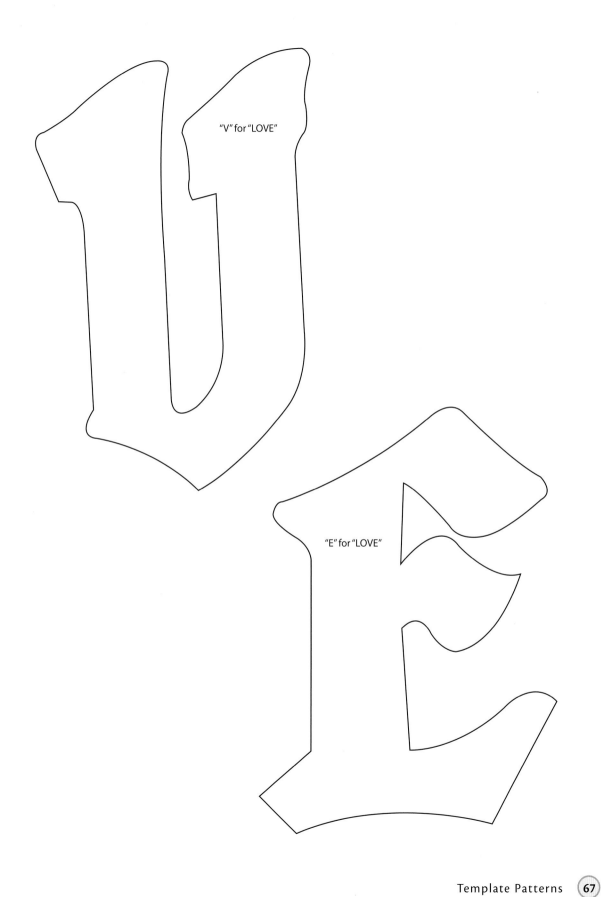

"V" for "LOVE"

"E" for "LOVE"

"O" for "BOO"

"B" for "BOO"

Small gift box

Fold line

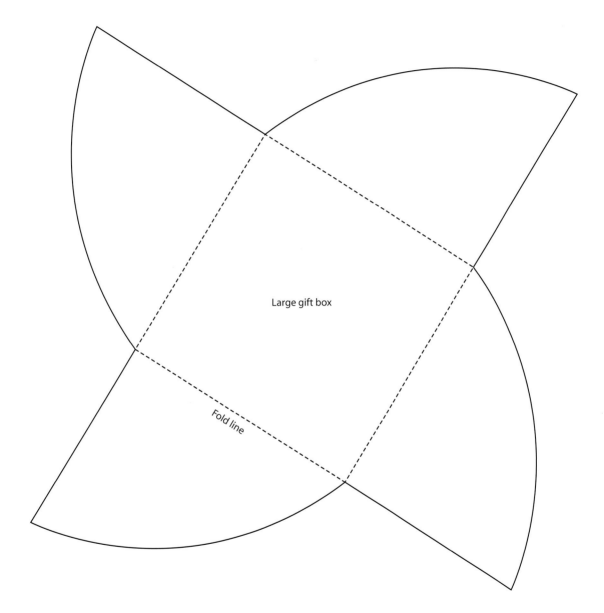

Large gift box

Fold line

# Room Decor
# and Fusible Fashions

Coordinate all those outfits with fusible fashions! Thin strips of interfacing with fused fabric can instantly change the look of a belt. Add elastic to small strips of fused fabric for a cute headband. Cut out those favorite fabric prints for darling pins. The options are limitless.

# Wearable Accessories

## BELTS

Each belt requires a thin strip of fast2fuse and fabric to wrap around both sides, along with a belt buckle. Use Shortcut 3, page 5 to fuse the fabric. The length and width of the belt depend on the size of the waist and the size of the buckle. Strips can be made longer by overlapping fast2fuse when pressing. Strips must be wide enough for individual buckles. Use hot glue to adhere the fabric around the main buckle. Use a paper punch to make holes on the belt. Glue on small belt loops, if desired.

## HEADBANDS

Use the headband pattern, page 83, and increase or decreased the size as needed. Use Shortcut 3, page 5, to fuse fabric to both sides of an appropriately sized piece of fast2fuse. Punch holes on both ends. Tie elastic through the holes, sizing the headband to the head.

## PINS

Fuse and cut small designs from fabric. Glue a pin onto the back. Apply coats of clear acrylic varnish to the top of the pin; high gloss works well. Many coats will add a glasslike finish to the pin.

**Extra Fun!**

Add embellishments, such as glitter, to the projects.

Make bracelets in a similar fashion as the headbands. You may want to use hook-and-loop tape.

Make an entire matching ensemble of items.

Highlight any table by adding coordinating placemats and napkin rings. Change fabrics for the holidays or create colorful faux patchwork designs. Napkin rings are simply fused strips of fabric glued into little tube shapes. fast2fuse is washable, so it's perfect for the table.

# Table Settings

## MATERIALS

*For 4 placemats 12" × 16"*

- 1 yard heavyweight fast2fuse
- 2 yards fabric
- Embellishments, such as rick-rack, braid, or ribbons (optional)
- Fabric glue (optional)
- Fusible appliqué web (optional)

## INSTRUCTIONS

*See General Directions for fast2fuse, page 4, for fusing directions.*

**1.** Use Shortcut 1, page 5, to fuse the fabric to both sides of the yard of fast2fuse.

**2.** Cut 4 rectangles, each 12" × 16", for placemats. Use scraps for napkin rings. If desired, add additional fabric layers, using fusible appliqué web.

**3.** Embellish as desired, making sure to use washable fabric glue.

**Extra Fun!**

Use fabric paint to write or stamp a message, such as, "Eat your veggies."

Fuse a different fabric to each side of the placemat.

Make napkins and napkin rings to match the placemats.

dding to decor is easier than ever with these quick, easy coasters! Fun for every season and holiday, they really are a snap to make.

# Coasters

## MATERIALS

*For 6 coasters*

- ¼ yard heavyweight fast2fuse

- 2 fabric pieces, ¼ yard each, with different patterns

- Fabric scraps for detail (optional)

- Fusible appliqué web (optional)

- Fabric glue (optional)

- Embellishments, such as fabric markers, lace, and ribbon (optional)

## INSTRUCTIONS

*All patterns for this chapter are on pages 77–83. Use a copy machine to enlarge the patterns 125%.*

*See General Directions for fast2fuse, page 4, for fusing directions.*

**1.** Use Shortcut 1, page 5, to fuse fabric to both sides of the fast2fuse.

**2.** Trace the patterns and cut out the shapes.

**3.** Add detail with fabric markers or use fusible appliqué web to add smaller pieces of fabric on top of the coaster shapes.

Use photo fabric for a coaster.

Make a funny coaster blob to look like a spill.

Make coasters that match the placemats.

H ighlight those beloved photos by adding a fabric mat or frame. Best made with a rotary cutter for super smooth lines, mats can make pictures really stand out!

# Frames and Mats

## MATERIALS

- Heavyweight fast2fuse of desired size
- Fabric to cover one side of fast2fuse
- Fabric glue and tape
- Rulers and marking tools

## INSTRUCTIONS

*See General Directions for fast2fuse, page 4, for fusing directions.*

**1.** Fuse only one side of the desired size of fast2fuse.

**2.** Trim the fabric.

**3.** Measure and cut out a window for the photo. The window opening must be at least ¼" smaller than the photo on all sides.

**4.** Glue or tape the photo to the back of the mat.

**5.** Insert the mat into the frame or glue the mat to a larger "frame" made from a rectangle of fused fast2fuse.

Glue a ribbon to the back of the mat for hanging.

Make a dimensional frame by layering rectangles of fused fabric.

Hang a series of little mats and photos together with a ribbon.

**K**eep craft supplies neat and orderly or keep that mail close at hand with this nifty organizer. Hang it on a closet door for easy access. Make several and string them together for even more room. These can be made in any size desired.

# Hanging Organizers

## MATERIALS

*For 1 organizer 12" × 16"*

- ½ yard heavyweight fast2fuse
- 1 yard fabric
- Low-heat glue gun with glue
- Paper punch (optional)
- Embellishments, such as rick-rack, lace, and ribbon (optional)
- Grommets (optional)

## INSTRUCTIONS

*See General Directions for fast2fuse, page 4, for fusing directions.*

**1.** Use Shortcut 1, page 5, to fuse the fabric to the fast2fuse. Cut a 12" × 16" rectangle for the organizer's main base.

**2.** Cut 2 rectangles 4" × 14". Fold in 1" flaps on both short ends.

**3.** Glue the 2 rectangles to the main base by putting glue along the bottom edge and on the flaps. Wrap the flaps around and secure them to the back of the organizer. This creates 2 pockets.

**4.** Add grommets to the top of the organizer for ease of hanging, if you like.

**5.** Embellish as desired.

**Extra Fun!**

Fill an organizer with useful items and give as a gift.

Store compact discs in an organizer.

Make a holiday-themed organizer to hold cards.

Nothing brightens up a room like flowers. These are easy to make and a fun way to use scraps. Make a bouquet or a table centerpiece or string them together for a flower garland or other wall decor. Use the patterns here or create new blossoms.

**Extra Fun!**

Curl the petals around a pencil for a fresh look.

Add safe tealights to the centers of the lilies or poinsettias.

Make a garland of flowers to string across a window.

# Flowers

## MATERIALS

*For 1 bouquet*

- ¼ yard heavyweight fast2fuse
- 3 fat quarters or fabric scraps
- Chenille strips (2 per flower)
- Fabric glue
- Embellishments, such as pom-poms, buttons, and lace (optional)

## INSTRUCTIONS

*All patterns for this chapter are on pages 77–83. Use a copy machine to enlarge the patterns 125%.*

*See General Directions for fast2fuse, page 4, for fusing directions.*

**1.** Cut the fast2fuse into pattern-sized rectangles.

**2.** Fuse the fabric, trace the patterns, and cut out.

**3.** Twist chenille strips 2 at a time to make stems. Glue the stems to the backs of the flowers.

**4.** Glue on pom-poms or button centers, if desired.

## Lily Pad or Poinsettia Centerpiece

Make these the same as the flowers except layer the smaller flowers inside the bigger flowers. Make a lily pad or napkin base.

# Template Patterns

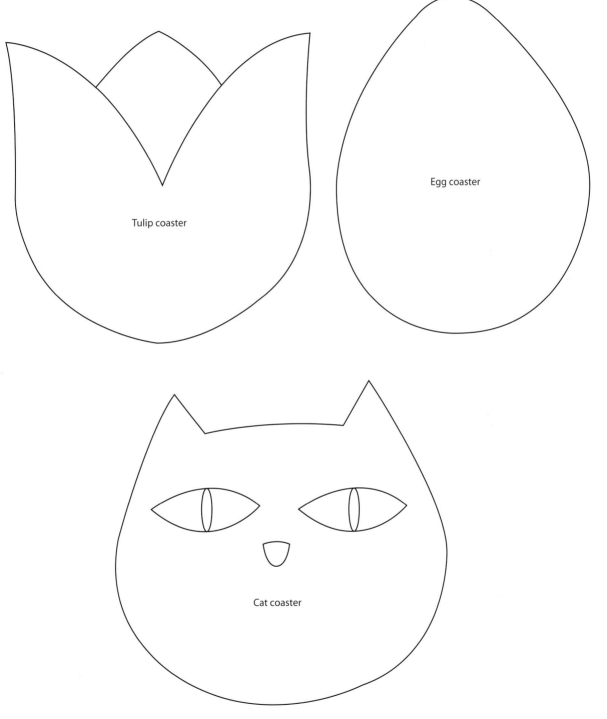

Tulip coaster

Egg coaster

Cat coaster

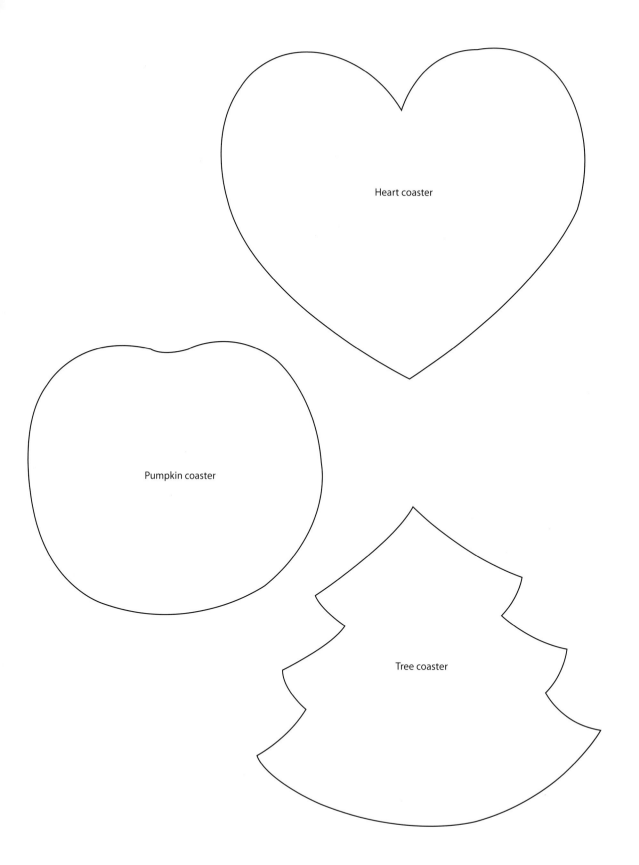

Heart coaster

Pumpkin coaster

Tree coaster

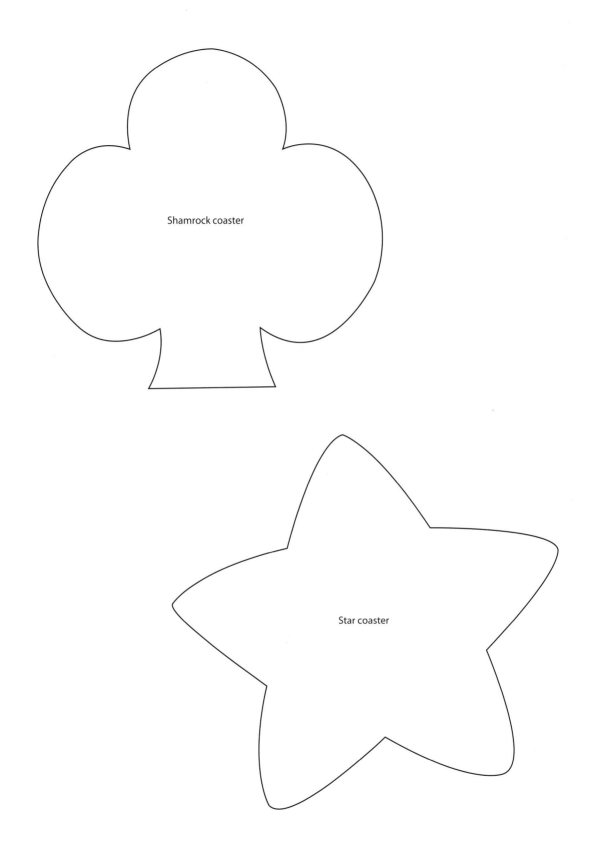

Shamrock coaster

Star coaster

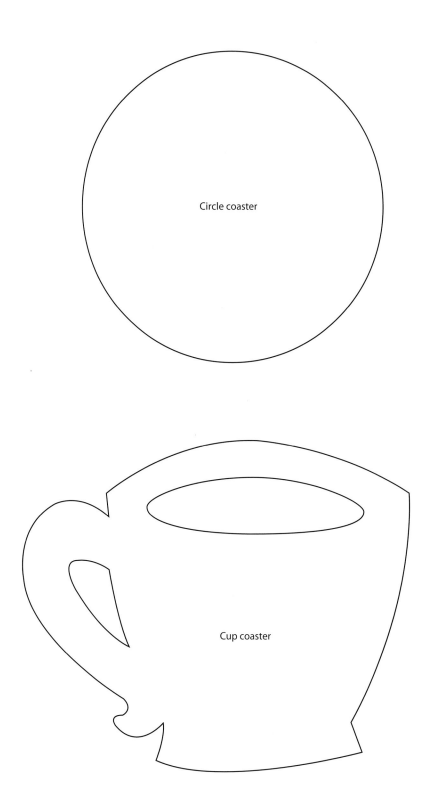

Circle coaster

Cup coaster

Flowers picks,
lily pads, poinsettias

Flowers picks,
lily pads, poinsettias

Flowers picks,
lily pads, poinsettias

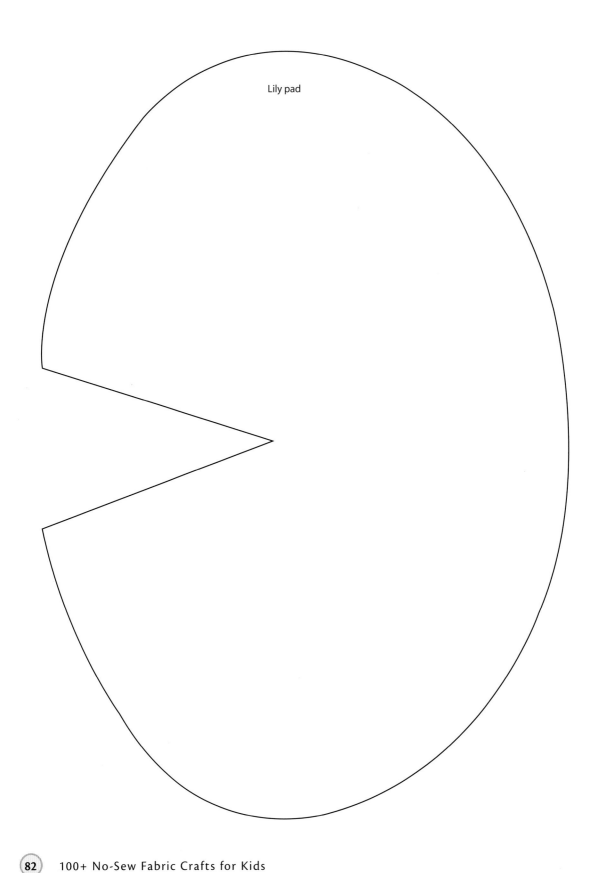

Lily pad

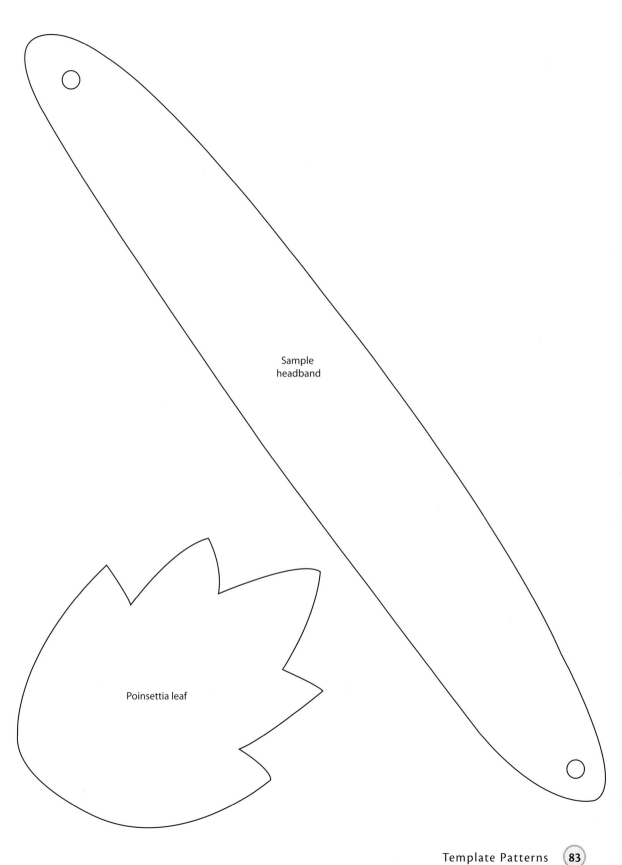

Sample
headband

Poinsettia leaf

# Holiday Goodies

**H**earts of all kinds are what this holiday of love is all about. Decorate a door with a banner or hang these darling hearts by ribbons. Add glitter to make things sparkle. Use scraps to make heart bouquets, pins, or cards!

# Valentine's Day

## MATERIALS

*For 1 "Hug" banner*

- ¼ yard heavyweight fast2fuse
- 2 or more fat quarters
- Fabric glue
- 24" ribbon of desired width (optional)
- Fabric marker (optional)
- Paper punch (optional)

## INSTRUCTIONS

*All patterns for this chapter are on pages 89–94. Use a copy machine to enlarge the patterns 125%.*

*See General Directions for fast2fuse, page 4, for fusing directions.*

**1.** Trace and cut out 3 large and 3 small hearts from fast2fuse.

**2.** Fuse the fabric to one side only of each heart.

**3.** Glue each small heart onto a large heart.

**4.** Write or stencil words such as *hug* or *luv*, if desired.

**5.** Glue hearts down a fused strip of fabric or a 24" strip of ribbon. Make a hole in the fabric strip or loop the ribbon to hang.

## Hanging Hearts

Use 2 fused hearts for each hanging heart, each with a different fabric. Then cut slots in each heart, one from the top to the middle and one from the bottom to the middle. Slide the hearts together and dab with glue to secure in place. Hang the hearts by the desired length of ribbon, tying a loop on one end and gluing the other end to the top of the heart.

**Extra Fun!**

Use scraps to make heart pins and magnets.

Send a special heart-shaped postcard.

Make heart picks to add to bouquets.

et ready for the spooky season with bats, mini witch hats, candy holders, and extra-scary coasters. Mini tombstones can be stuck in a cake or bread pan filled with yummy treats. These small projects are perfect for scraps and odds and ends.

**Extra Fun!**

String scary shapes together for a fun garland.

Mini witch hats can hold place cards or be turned upside down to hold treats.

Make scary masks from fast2fuse.

# Halloween

## MATERIALS

### For 3 bats

- ¼ yard heavyweight fast2fuse
- ½ yard fabric
- Embellishments, such as googly eyes and pom-poms
- Fabric glue
- Scraps of fur (optional)
- String for hanging (optional)

## INSTRUCTIONS

*All patterns for this chapter are on pages 89–94. Use a copy machine to enlarge the patterns 125%.*

*See General Directions for fast2fuse, page 4, for fusing directions.*

**1.** Use Shortcut 1, page 5, to fuse the fabric to the fast2fuse.

**2.** Trace and cut out 3 bats.

**3.** Glue a small piece of fur to the middle of each bat. Glue on the eyes and nose.

**4.** Make a tiny hole along one wing and hang by a loop of string.

## Mini Witch Hats

Mini witch hats are made like the cone party hats, page 54, except a small ring is made for a hat brim.

## Candy Cones

Candy cones are made from the small witch hat pattern. Glue on some trim and maybe a small corded handle.

## Coasters

Coasters are made like the Fabulous Flats, page 7. The scary hand coaster is a self-traced hand.

N othing says spring like pastel colors and eggs. Add white bunnies to the mix and get ready for Easter. The wreath is simply colorful eggs arranged in a circle. The bunny box can hold dyed eggs or jelly beans and other treats. Candy cones can hold jellybeans or even serve as little purses.

**Extra Fun!**

Make egg-shaped placemats from fast2fuse.

Make egg-shaped invitations.

Make candy cones or purse cones from the cone hat pattern, page 61.

# Easter

## Egg Wreath Materials

- ⅓ yard heavyweight fast2fuse
- Array of colorful fabric scraps
- ⅓ yard ribbon
- Fabric glue
- Large (10″) dinner plate for template
- Small (6″) dessert plate for template

## Egg Wreath Instructions

*All patterns for this chapter are on pages 89–94. Use a copy machine to enlarge the patterns 125%.*

*See General Directions for fast2fuse, page 4, for fusing directions.*

**1.** Use the 2 plates to trace a 2″-wide circle of fast2fuse for the wreath. Cut out the wreath. Trace and cut out as many eggs as possible from the remaining fast2fuse.

**2.** Fuse one side of each egg. Trim the edges.

**3.** Arrange the eggs in a circle around the wreath; glue to secure.

**4.** Glue a loop of ribbon to the back of the wreath for hanging.

## Bunny Box Materials

8″ × 10″ rectangle of heavyweight fast2fuse

2 fabric scraps 8½″ × 10½″ (1 white and 1 colorful)

Fabric glue

Embellishments, such as buttons, pom-poms, and fabric markers

12″ trim (optional)

## Bunny Box Instructions

*All patterns for this chapter are on pages 89–94. Use a copy machine to enlarge the patterns 125%.*

*See General Directions for fast2fuse, page 4, for fusing directions.*

**1.** Use Shortcut 1, page 5, to fuse white fabric to one side of the fast2fuse and colorful fabric to the other.

**2.** Trace the pattern and cut out.

**3.** Crease along the fold lines and glue at the tabs.

**4.** Add a nose, eyes, and other trim as desired.

**D**eck the halls with trees, candy cane reindeer, cute mice, and gingerbread men. These small items can be made using scraps. Go all out with the embellishments and make them sparkle!

Make three-dimensional trees of all sizes by shrinking or enlarging the pattern.

A gingerbread bear would make a cute holiday greeting card or invitation. Stamp, print, or glue information on the back of the bear.

# Christmas

## MATERIALS

- Pattern-sized rectangles of fast2fuse
- Fabric scraps
- Fabric glue
- Invisible thread (optional)
- Embellishments, such as fabric markers, pom-poms, and chenille strips (optional)
- Candy canes (optional)

## INSTRUCTIONS

*All patterns for this chapter are on pages 89–94. Use a copy machine to enlarge the patterns 125%.*

*See General Directions for fast2fuse, page 4, for fusing directions.*

**1.** Use Shortcut 1, page 5, to fuse the fabric to the fast2fuse.

**2.** Trace the patterns and cut out.

**3.** Embellish as desired. Glue a loop of invisible thread for hanging.

### Reindeer

Each reindeer is made by gluing 2 fused heads together, with candy cane or chenille antlers sandwiched and glued in between. Leave the sides unglued to slide a candy cane into the eating reindeer.

### Mouse and Wreath

This ornament has its pieces stacked for dimension. Start with the feet, then add the wreath, then the head and paws.

### Gingerbread Bear

Simply fuse and cut. The more embellishments, the better.

### Three-Dimensional Trees

Two slotted tree pieces are needed for each. Cut one tree's slot from the top to the middle and the other's from the bottom to the middle. Slide the 2 trees together and dot with glue to secure, if desired.

### Cone Bouquet Holder

This is simply a cone party hat from page 54. Glue a loop of ribbon to the back for hanging. Fill the cone with your favorite holiday picks and candy canes. Shrink the pattern to make small cone tree ornaments to be filled with treats, tiny toys, or small holiday picks.

# Template
# Patterns

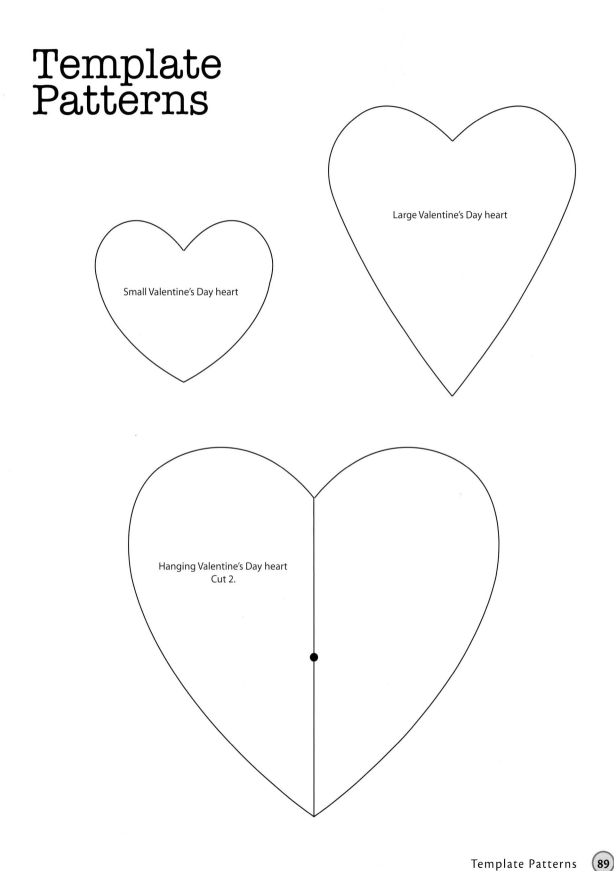

Large Valentine's Day heart

Small Valentine's Day heart

Hanging Valentine's Day heart
Cut 2.

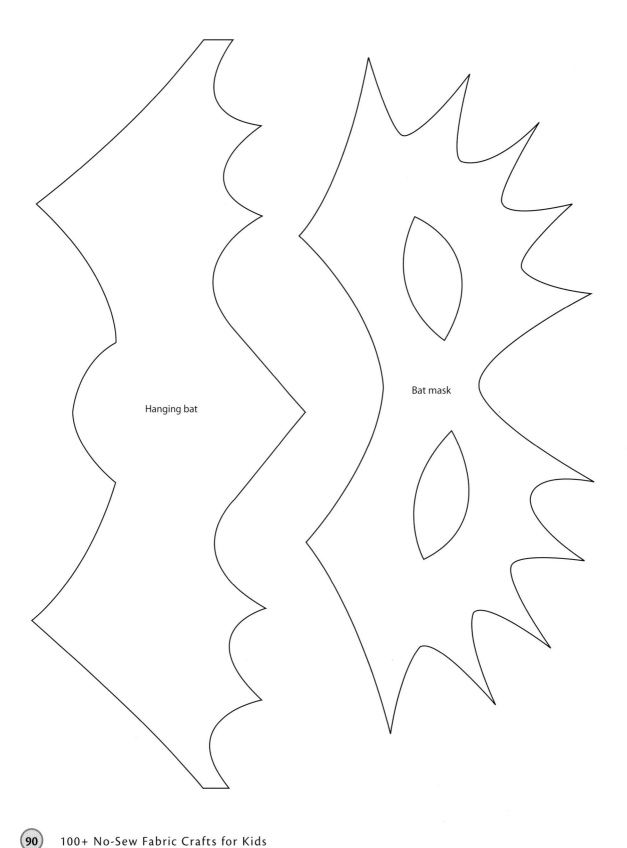

Hanging bat

Bat mask

Ghost for tombstone

Mini witch hat

Bat pin

Skull coaster

R I P

Tombstone

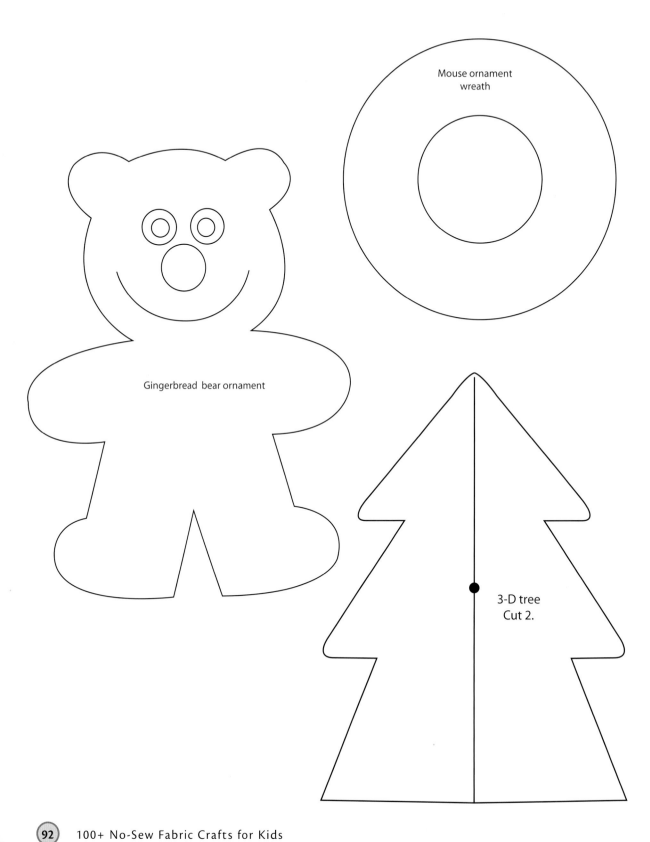

Mouse ornament
wreath

Gingerbread bear ornament

3-D tree
Cut 2.

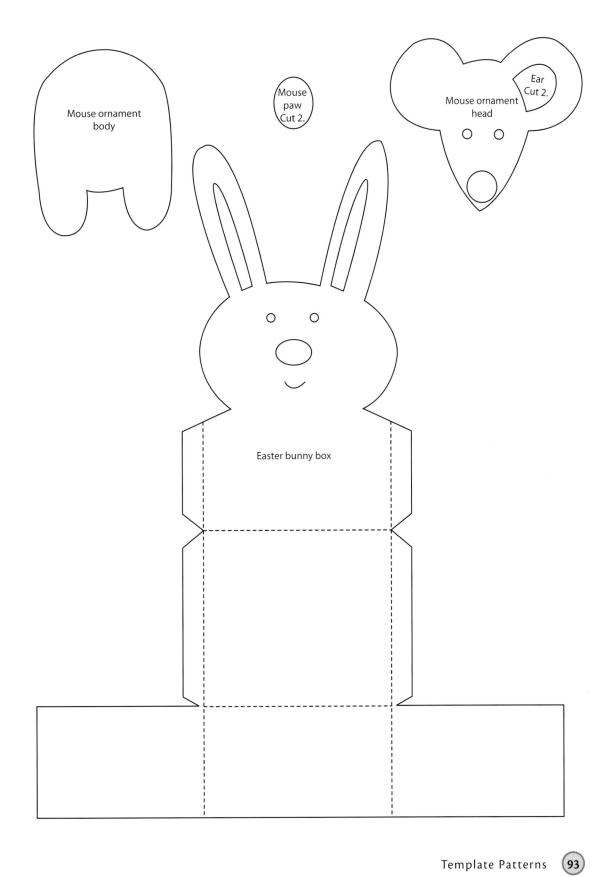

Mouse ornament body

Mouse paw Cut 2.

Mouse ornament head

Ear Cut 2.

Easter bunny box

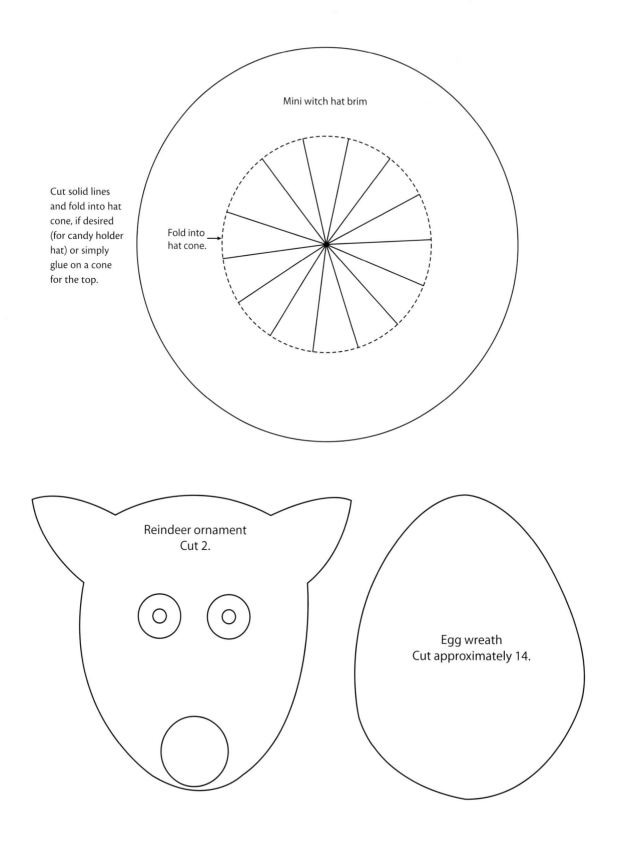

Mini witch hat brim

Cut solid lines
and fold into hat
cone, if desired
(for candy holder
hat) or simply
glue on a cone
for the top.

Fold into
hat cone.

Reindeer ornament
Cut 2.

Egg wreath
Cut approximately 14.

# About the Author

**M**ary Link is an experienced artist and crafts-person. Although she has worked with a variety of materials, from stained glass to wood, Mary finds fabric art to be one of the most satisfying. Whether sewing quilts, clothes, costumes, or crafts, Mary enjoys the flexibility that fabric provides. She also enjoys sharing that love of fabric with children and adults.

Mary lives in St. Paul, Minnesota, with her husband and sons. She encourages everyone to embrace their creative spirit . . . beginning with fabric!

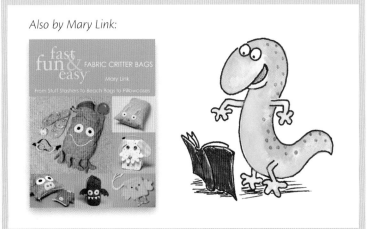

*Also by Mary Link:*

# Great Titles *from* C&T PUBLISHING

*Available at your local retailer or* **www.ctpub.com** *or* **800.284.1114**

*For a list of other fine books from C&T Publishing,*
*ask for a free catalog:*

**C&T PUBLISHING, INC.**

P.O. Box 1456

*Lafayette, CA 94549*

(800) 284-1114

*Email: ctinfo@ctpub.com*

*Website: www.ctpub.com*

*C&T Publishing's professional photography*
*services are now available to the public. Visit us*
*at www.ctmediaservices.com.*

*For quilting supplies:*

**COTTON PATCH**

*1025 Brown Ave.*

*Lafayette, CA 94549*

Store: (925) 284-1177

Mail order: (925) 283-7883

*Email: CottonPa@aol.com*

*Website: www.quiltusa.com*

*Note: Fabrics used in the quilts shown may not be currently*
*available, as fabric manufacturers keep most fabrics in*
*print for only a short time.*